A SOLDIER'S SILENCE

T.C. Grantham

A catalogue record for this book is available from the British Library.

Published by Goldcrest Books International Ltd
www.goldcrestbooks.com
publish@goldcrestbooks.com

ISBN: 978-1-913719-86-9

To my husband, without his support and encouragement this book would never have been finished.

PROLOGUE

Sidney Gains

Sleep did not come easily for me, my mind took everything in, and I felt the need to process everything around me, recycling each thought, every minute. It was late, or early, rather. At this point I wasn't sure if knowing the time would be better or worse. I listened to the waves crashing on the shore outside my open window. The steady ebb and flow was like a lullaby until the steadiness changed. I could now hear the light dinging bell of the buoy accompanied by a slight breeze that tickled the small hairs on my arm. The air was thick with the smell of the sea, I could feel it, its own entity that came in with the breeze. Thick and damp, I knew a fog was rolling in. I shifted to the sound of my white gossamer curtains blowing in and out as if the room was breathing; two dancing ghosts in the night. I focused on my breathing, on each body part, trying to manually relax my muscles and quiet my mind.

As I focused on the air coming in and leaving my lungs, I became hyperaware of a sound, breathing, but not my own. Someone else was in the room with me. My eyes flew open to the darkness just as a clammy hand clapped down over my mouth.

My fight or flight response had already kicked in, but I was not fast enough. Before I had a chance to move, he was on top of me, pinning my arms to my sides. Being in the military, I had been trained, hours of training. In this situation it didn't mean anything because I was going up against one of my own; he was equally trained but just enough stronger that he matched me move by move. I stopped fighting, in a battle of wits I knew I could win, I needed information, so I pretended to give up. I quit struggling and focused my eyes on his face, I knew it was him before our eyes had met. I knew his smell, his hands, his breath. We stared at each other briefly until my gaze darted to the wall where the control panel was, he knew right where I was looking and why. The light was red, red; then why was he here, and how? The door to his cell was still locked yet here he was, on top of me, gaining control. He leaned his face down to mine, his breath hot and thick.

"Good morning, Doc, you're not too shocked, are you? Because I could leave and try that again."

He chortled and leaned his head back; I could barely see the crooked mischievous smile on his face through the darkness. I caught a glimpse of his teeth, yellowed from years of neglect. His hand was so tight over my mouth it was making it hard to breathe. I was fighting against panic and hoped he couldn't read it on my face. Sid had been my patient now for almost a year. I had been playing around in his brain, I knew him. It appeared that a thousand thoughts could move through my brain in a single second, but I couldn't get them in order, I was still panicking. He thought he was reading me, giving off an air of confidence. I knew it was nothing more than a cover, the sheen of sweat on his face, his hands cold and clammy, he was scared. I closed my eyes briefly and tried to take a deep breath. Patience would be my weapon, I needed to keep him talking, make him believe I had conceded. He would make a mistake and I would be ready.

"Don't try to figure it out, Doc," he said, reading my mind. "You'll just end up all sorts of screwed in that pretty little head of yours."

He held a gun in his hand and gestured it to his temple, and laughed hysterically, almost as though it was a rehearsed play. He was putting on a show for me. why? He took the gun and pressed it hard to my head. It was cold, I could smell the oil and metal.

"Now, if I take my hand off of your mouth, do you promise to be good?"

His voice squeaked at the end, leading into a short mocking laugh.

"Wait, you can't answer, maybe I should abandon the plan altogether. I mean, thinking of you and screwed in the same sentence sounds kinda nice, Doc, are you up for a late-night romp in the sheets?"

He traced the gun from my temple down to my cheek, never letting up. I could feel my skin stretching with the pressure and I tried not to wince. He tucked the gun in the waist of his pants, I thought that would be my moment. His eyes raged; he knew what I was thinking.

"I wouldn't if I were you, Doc, even if you win this battle, you will lose the war."

As much as I hated it, he intrigued me, I wanted to know what he was talking about.

"Now, let's try this again, you'll be quiet, won't you?" he asked.

He let the pressure off my mouth ever so slightly but kept my mouth covered. I was grateful to be able to take a deep breath. My breathing became heavier as he ran his fingers down my neck to my chest, in one quick movement he snapped open a button on my shirt exposing the top of my breasts. A chill of fear ran up my spine, the thought of Sidney Gains anywhere near my body was enough to almost make me lose my cool, almost. His eyes stared at my newly exposed skin, and he shuddered.

"Well?" he asked, and his tongue traced the outline of his lips, then bit his bottom lip. I nodded my head a slow and steady 'yes' as best I could. He leaned in close again and whispered, "Good, " his hot breath saturating my ear. At the point my jaw was screaming against the pressure, he let loose, and I opened and closed my mouth to stretch the sore muscles.

"Don't do that, Doc, I am already fighting all kinds of urges, but you're for him."

"Sid, what is going on, I don't understand."

He cut me off.

"That is the beauty of this, Doc, you will never understand, just try and wrap your head around the fact that it is as it is meant to be. You're out, Doc, well, I guess technically I am out but who's counting. And the main thing and trust me it will give you the shits later, is, what you could have done to prevent this, nothing. And what you did wrong, everything."

I could only hope that he believed he had won, that I had given up. In fact, he was following my plan to keep him talking, at some point his monologue would distract him just long enough for me to make a move. I refused to go down without a fight, it's not me, not ever. I would get out of this or die trying. As much as I wanted to just get away from him, I needed information, whatever I could manipulate out of him.

"Sid, you've come so far. Why?"

He cut me off again, laughing.

"*Please*, don't think for one second your mind screwing had any sort of effect on me beyond wanting to slap the shit out of your perfect little face."

I tested his position on my body, I tried ever so slightly to move without him feeling what I was doing. He sat on my chest and pinned my body down. If I could get him to lean forward, even a little, I might be able to use my legs against him. I had momentarily tuned him out, but Sid was still talking, muttering about some disgusting thing he wanted to do to me. I was taking in my surroundings. My gun in the drawer of the nightstand, the control to his prisoner implant on my lapel in the closet, although I couldn't imagine it would work considering he got out of a locked cell. Wait, before, he said *him*...who was he talking about?

"Sid, you are too strong for this, why are you letting this person control you?"

"Let him? You stupid bitch, let him? I asked him to."

Just then I felt him shift, all in one second my mind screamed at my body: go, now!" I slammed my feet into the bed lifting my hips up, jolting Sidney forward, our faces just inches apart. I flung my legs upward, wrapping them from behind around his neck. Then, with all my strength, I threw him backward. As I had hoped, Sidney was not expecting it and tumbled off the bed, his gun skidding across the room. He landed on his feet, stumbled back, then fell to his butt on the floor. He quickly jumped up but found himself face to face with the barrel of my gun.

"Do not move, Sid, my only issue with killing you is that I don't want to get blood on my rug."

He lifted his hands slowly and calculatingly and put them on his head. That crooked smile was back, and he was nodding in approval. I half expected him to offer me applause, instead he began to laugh.

"Shut up, Sidney!" I yelled.

I had had enough of it; I was ready for the night to be over. My mind was reeling, I wanted so much to process everything, that day, the week, the last year that he had been there. His laughter did not die but he kneeled and began to lie face down on the floor keeping his hands positioned behind his head. I kept my gun on him and kicked his gun hard, and it skidded under my dresser across the room. I grabbed my satellite phone off the wall; dispatch immediately picked up.

"How can we help, Major Giles?" the voice on the

other end said. My voice was shaky, but I did not leave out a single detail of what had just happened.

"Is the inmate currently subdued?" the voice asked.

"Yes," I replied. "I have a gun trained on him."

"Are you safe, Major?"

Am I safe? That was a question I didn't think I could answer. I thought I was safe, though now I was not sure what safe meant. Instead, I answered: "The inmate has been apprehended, please send me some backup."

"Officers are on their way."

It didn't take long to hear the sirens approaching. I didn't speak, I didn't listen, I just stood there, empty, with my gun pointed at his head. Sidney was taunting me by singing "Row Your Boat" and the itsy-bitsy spider Song.

"I said *shut up*, Sid."

"Oh, poor doctor, can't have any fun." He ridiculed.

I crouched down over him and grabbed a fist-full of hair, pulling his face to look at mine. Just as our eyes met, he spat in my face. It was instinct, I used the butt of my gun and slammed him in the back of my head, knocking him unconscious. My ears started ringing, I think the adrenaline was wearing off and my body wasn't thrilled with what it had just been through. I took a few deep breaths, hearing the sirens louder and the cars pulling down my driveway. The ringing in my ears had stopped and a voice came to my mind.

"Major Giles, can you hear me? Major?"

My eyes focused on his.

"It's okay, we've got this."

I briefly saw his eyes dart to my chest; I hadn't realized

my shirt was still gaping open. I pulled my shirt closed, my gun still tightly gripped in my other hand. I sat on the edge of my bed. What followed was an onslaught of questions, which to my confusion and shame I could not answer. Sid was silent on the floor, bound at his ankles and hands. I wasn't sure if he was awake yet, he lay there unmoving. I must admit that scared me more than his words or his laughter. I felt like I was the next act in a complex play, and I knew somehow that it wasn't over. My calm, serene bedroom now looked like a crime scene. Red and blue lights, yellow tape, flashing camera bulbs, and soldiers everywhere. I sat there alone, holding my shirt and my gun, while an emergency medical technician started shining a flashlight in my eyes and asking questions, I flinched away, dismissing the care.

"I'm fine, okay. Just get him out of here, would you?"

I shifted my eyes to Gains, watching his every move while they lifted him off the floor. I could see now that he was awake, his eyes darted in my direction and a sly smile spread across his face as they carted him away. I didn't take my eyes off him until he was out of sight. He never once struggled. My only thought was, "This isn't over." I said it quietly to myself, then again in my head.

"What?" I asked, annoyed, when I realized someone had said my name probably more than once.

"How do you feel, Major Giles?" the EMT asked again.

"I'm fine," I snapped, gathered my wits and repeated in a kinder tone, "I am fine, thank you. He didn't hurt me; I just really want to get my house back and process whatever the hell just happened here. I want diagnostics, a full panel," I started, then realizing my error said, "Sorry, that's not your job."

The EMT shrugged and reluctantly walked away and busied herself with other tasks. Military officers and local police hovered around the room. I sat silently taking it all in, the past, the present, and what was going to happen in the future.

"Major Giles?" I looked up to see a soldier holding the gun Sid had used. He was tall, with a broad build and very dark hair. He had a crooked nose, but it looked good on him. "Was your weapon fired?" he asked.

"No, sir, it wasn't, this is my gun." I gestured to the gun still in my hand.

"Odd," he muttered, "this is a military weapon, if you have your gun, do you know where he would have gotten it?" He eyed me subjectively.

"Of course, not, Major, what are you getting at?"

"Listen, I am going to have to get your statement in writing, you will need to come down to the station within twenty-four hours. We still have some documenting to do. I am sorry, Major, we will try and get out of your hair soon."

I reassured the soldier that I would be in to give my statement. I went over it once more in my head, memorizing every word. It started to feel robotic, as though I was talking about someone else, just telling a story. I wasn't sure if it was good that I had disconnected myself from this already; that seemed to be a habit of mine. He wasn't asked any more questions, but he swabbed my hands for gunshot residue took some blood samples to make sure

I wasn't on any drugs or alcohol, then took the security tape from my cameras. I finally stood, after what seemed like forever, and set my gun on my bedside table; I walked over to my closet. I pulled on a sweatshirt. That same crooked-nosed soldier cleared his throat behind me.

"Major, I need you to sign this promise to appear. I will give you a copy, the address is."

"I know where to go," I said, a bit too snarkily, judging by the look on his face.

He glanced at my bedside table and back at me.

"Don't forget to bring your gun." He bit back the sarcasm dripping in his tone. I thought under different circumstances we could have been friends.

"I'm sorry, soldier," I asked, "what was your name? Sorry if you already told me."

He hesitated briefly, then smiled.

"Major Hank Jackson," he replied.

I smiled, trying to smooth things over with Major Jackson, and signed the documents. I stood and waited while people filed out slowly after finishing their given jobs, with the shuffling of their footsteps fading into the distance.

Once everyone had gone, I sat on the edge of my bed in silence. I had no idea what time it was or how long this whole thing had lasted. Extreme tiredness suddenly washed over me; I was finally alone. I felt strange, like my home wasn't my home any longer, it felt violated and unsafe. I stood up and started pulling blankets and pillows off the bed. I stripped it down to the mattress, throwing the blankets and pillows and sheets in a pile in the corner.

I then walked from room to room, counting every step while my hand ran over the furniture, and checking every lock. I wasn't sure if I was making amends or making up things to do to occupy my mind. I went back to my room and sat on the edge of my bare mattress, the sounds and smells were different now; I wondered if it would always feel different. My eyes were tired, my body wasn't numb but tingly and strange. My mind focused, I started down the path I was trying to avoid, not the nitty-gritty details the military would want, but the emotion, his face, the way I felt, what I could have done. What I should have done. My mind pulled to the biggest detail, my biggest feign, my part in the play, my gun. It was there sitting on my bedside table where I had left it. I reached over and picked it up, turning it around in my hands; it felt too light. Even with everything that had happened I smiled. I opened the drawer to my bedside table, took out a fully loaded clip and inserted it into my empty gun.

Chapter 1

Alone

My name is Presley Giles, I am a major and a doctor in the United States Army Special Forces. I have my PhD in medicine and psychiatry. My job is to work closely with soldiers who need rehabilitation; I work mostly with psychiatric patients but so often the body is broken too. For almost half of my life the world has been at war. It started fifteen years ago and long since became the third World War. So many countries tried to stay out of it, without realizing they were already in it. Year after year more were forced to pick a side, some countries were literally torn apart. Russia and China banded together, secretly placing their pawns, it came like a flash of lightning when they started it. There was talk of conspiracy for years, most pushed it off as just that. Conspiracy. The truth is they had infiltrated our country, our military, right under our noses. We believe they had been planning it for decades. The US fought back to protect its allies along with its own, and now, it seems the world consists of just two conjoined, warring countries, and those lines often still seem blurred. It is easy to forget who goes where, or who you can trust.

I live in a white stucco mansion with an orange terracotta tile roof, on an island off the coast of Belize. It is surrounded by a tall, gray stone fence that encases three sides of the property, with a large, black, twisted iron gate at the front. It has a long cobblestone drive; I can almost imagine how, years before, the sound of horses' hooves would echo off the stone walls, pulling big, beautiful coaches behind them. A large, circular fountain with an old copper seahorse, green from age and weather, that spouted water from its head sat near the front door. The house is located on the beach, the main bedroom was built up on a pier foundation, so the waves come right up to the house during high tide. With such a large, sprawling property, I felt like I was in my own little world and able to almost forget what was going on outside those gates. Most places operated normally, but there were places where the war is still very much raging on. We pretend, but I don't think the fear is very far off from anyone's thoughts. I wondered how I was so lucky to have lived here these past few years. The home was seized years ago from a family with questionable business dealings; at times I can almost imagine the drug lords skulking around the house. Soon after it was seized, it was equipped with the latest security system and made into a prison and a medical facility. A lot of the patients I work with here are dangerous and most have committed crimes, and oftentimes they come to me physically wounded in some way.

I feel hidden away here, which I like. From the outside I might look like a wealthy widow, however, the large American flag and the red medical flag I have flying in the middle of the courtyard outside tells their own tales to any on-lookers who might wonder. On the inside, it serves as a high-security, state-of-the-art rehabilitation facility. I prefer to refer to the inmates as my patients, it seems less like I am accusing them and more like I am here to help.

I was alone, alone with my thoughts and my plants. For someone who cares for others and is rarely alone, being alone never bothered me, I get used to it quickly when it happens, and I welcome it.

My patients tended to make poor company, and I kept them at arm's length to keep things strictly professional. For me, the idea of any level of companionship went out the window years ago. I knew I would live and die for the job. At least I knew I could die saying I did my part to find peace in the world and that I gave what I could to bring some light to the darkness. I decided a long time ago that love was of fairy tales and romance novels. I found love in other places, my favorite room in the house was the greenhouse, and I spent any free time I might have in there; my plants serve as wonderful distractions. They live, they breathe, and offer me their beauty and richness, a symbiotic relationship, which I value greatly.

I sat in the greenhouse with my eyes closed, taking in the damp air, the smell of wet dirt dancing through my nostrils, I took a deep breath. It had been two weeks since Sid had been taken away. As much as I tried to avoid it, every now and then my mind drifted to the things that happened that night. I had to fight to assure myself that I had done everything I could and that I hadn't done anything wrong. I hadn't heard anything about him, in past instances that would usually have meant he had been executed. I had requested not to know about such things, ignorance really can be bliss when dealing with other's lives.

The glass walls glittered with water droplets, I stood from my stool, watering can in hand, and began lovingly feeding my babies. Plants of all sorts lined a walkway, sitting on long wooden tables, and beautiful flowering vines cascaded from pots hanging from the ceiling. I walked from plant-to-plant, showering each with water and speaking kind words. All my worries melted away when I had purpose.

I hadn't received any new patients, but it didn't bother me this time, I think I needed the time to process and heal, my ego more than anything. I jokingly said to myself, "I'm getting too old for this." At twenty-seven I was still in my prime, but anything over thirteen is too old for drama, and Sidney Gains was drama. Still, I wandered the house day by day, tending to my plants, coming back to terms with myself and my surroundings. I admit I had found a bit of normalcy in my solitude these last couple of weeks. It is refreshing to not expect anything or have anything expected of you.

That morning when I woke up the beach was calling me, beckoning me to its sand as a means of escape. I finished with my plants and went to my bedroom and changed my clothes. I stretched my back and each leg, then laced up my running shoes. My body was giddy with the idea as I headed down my back steps to the beach, I could feel the adrenaline building and I was off. The sound of my feet hitting the wet sand was therapeutic, my heartbeat steady like my footfall, and the waves crashing nearby all in a rhythm like a dance. I had run the distance from home to the rocky shore near the lighthouse many times. I stopped and braced myself on my knees taking a few deep breaths. I stretched my legs and looked, squinting in the sun up at the lighthouse, it was close to noon now and I turned to head back toward home. I could see my house in the distance, and as I drew closer, I could see people standing on the back deck. The pounding in my ears changed just a bit, enough to make me realize the silhouettes standing there made me nervous.

I didn't slow my stride as I approached. Once I got a few yards away I could see that it was Colonel Weaver, my supervising officer, with two other soldiers that I hadn't seen before. Colonel Weaver was a tall, slender but muscular man, with wavy dark blonde hair and pale blue-gray eyes. A jagged scar ran down the left side of his face almost touching his eye and ending just above his jawline. He had a handsome face, very straight and symmetrical, his features made the scar seem more distinguished and attractive, mysterious, in a way. He stood with his legs shoulder distance apart, hands clasped behind him, the other soldiers flanked his right and left. His eyes narrowed as I approached.

I had spoken with Colonel Weaver many times over

the phone or by video call, however, rarely in person. The truth is, he was known to be a womanizer, women fell over themselves to go out with him, talk to him, be in his presence. Although I could appreciate a good-looking man, it did little to sway me to him. I hadn't been like that with him, or anyone, for as long as I could remember. He always seemed so passive or nonchalant around me, I assumed it bothered him that I didn't cling to his every word and therefore he didn't like me much. As I jogged up the stairs, I felt his eyes on me, but it was not just that his stare cut through me like ice all the way to my core. As he looked me up and down, my heart leaped in a way I was not familiar with, and my cheeks flushed with heat.

"Major Giles," was all he said, with a polite nod, and a crooked smile playing at the corners of his mouth, then he abruptly turned and walked into the house. I wasn't used to being under-dressed, or rather, out of uniform. I quickly fussed over my hair in the reflection of the glass and strode in after them. Just as I was walking in Colonel Weaver tossed a towel at me, more forcefully than I was expecting. It hit me awkwardly in my chest and I was barely able to catch it.

"Why don't you go clean up before we talk." He scratched at his scar, looking at me in a way that made my heart speed up. I didn't waste any time and started walking toward my bedroom when he said, "And Major, hurry." That crooked smile was back, something was different in the way he was interacting with me. I felt like I was in middle school and he was going to ask me to the dance.

Without saying anything, I hurried down the hall and into my room. I quickly dressed in uniform and twisted my hair into a low knot. I ran my hands down my sides as if to iron out any wrinkles and glanced in the mirror. I saw a collared, white, button-down shirt covered by a navy blue fitted blazer with crisp gold cording down the sleeves and around the cuffs. My calf-length pencil skirt and navy-blue heels completed the ensemble.

"That will have to do," I muttered to myself and walked out into the foyer. The sound of my heels on the tile floor seemed to echo and bounce off the walls. Colonel Weaver was standing with his back to me, staring out the window toward the sea. At first, the sound of my approach didn't touch him. Then, in an instant, he seemed very aware that I was there and he walked over to me quickly, quickly enough that I felt my insides flinch. He got close to me, more so than would have been acceptable in a normal conversation, and I didn't have enough time to be uncomfortable before he reached for my hand. I tightened my grasp around his in a good handshake then was surprised when he lifted our hands to his mouth, kissing my hand, and staring at me with intense eyes.

"It has been too long, Major, since I was in your presence," he said with a cadence in his tone that made me feel strange. He smiled at me, still holding my hand in his. I can only hope I hid the shock and confusion of his actions from showing on my face. I was instantly reminded of the first time I had met Colonel Weaver, back then a lieutenant and me a fresh new face. He was surrounded by four or five women, laughing and flirting.

I remembered him resting his arm on the shoulder of one of the women, with his jacket flung over his own shoulder, his white shirt too tight, showing off his muscles, no scar yet. I remembered trying to avoid the scene altogether and praying I wouldn't have to be involved with any of them. Considering that I am not a very sociable person I am surprised I had the desire to join the military; I wanted to help people, but I suppose it was lack of options that drove the decision. A few years later, I had finally graduated from my doctorate program, and Weaver had become some war hero. There was always talking and whispering about his last deployment, but I hadn't cared enough to get the details, I assumed it would all be hearsay anyway.

"So, how can I help you today, Colonel Weaver? This is a surprise." To say the least.

I maintained my composure, inwardly cringing as I remembered the past.

"Isn't it though?" He laughed a short, soft laugh. "A surprise, I mean. I have a new one for you, a real doozy," he said. A sly smile ran like slime over his face. He had such a way with words, I was beginning to understand why women found him so fascinating.

"Are you up to the task, Major?" he asked, snapping me out of my daydream.

A knot twisted in my stomach. I was unsure of the feelings behind it, was it him, or was it his words? I would write it off as being excited for a new patient, after all, I knew I was good at what I did, there was no question. I was often told that I have a way with people.

"Of course, Colonel. I am ready." He interrupted me

with a booming laugh. I flinched back a little and it didn't go unnoticed, a new fire burned in his gray eyes.

"Perfect," was all he said. That same slimy smile was back, but this time it didn't touch his eyes.

"I will send for him immediately." He turned on his heel and headed for the door waving for the two soldiers to follow him. "Expect him tomorrow morning."

He left as quickly and as strangely as he had come, and I was alone. It felt odd, and creepy, and another emotion that I couldn't quite explain.

Shortly after, even before the strangeness had worn off, I heard the familiar whirring of my fax machine spitting out pages. I had assumed Colonel Weaver was sending over my new patient files. Before I had even gotten to my office desk in my bedroom the machine had stopped, beeping to signal it was done. I waited for a few minutes, but nothing more came through. Three pages, that was it? Where was the rest? Just then the machine started again and spat out a single page, from Colonel Weaver. Keeping in sync with the strange events of the day he had written: *"Get him to talk"* followed by, *"Good Luck."* with his signature sprawled at the bottom. All I had were these three pages to go on. The first was a short recap of the patient's childhood to when he joined the military. It read like so many others, *Name: Captain William Miller Special Forces.* With a strange sort of emphasis on the abusive father, and absent mother, it didn't say if she had died, enlisted or just deserted him, only that she was absent. He had enlisted young; I assumed younger than was allowed. Page two was unsettling, just a list of all the people he had killed, their names, the dates and how they had been killed. Judging by the list, I had to assume he was a sniper, although those weren't usually included as crimes. It read more like a grocery list. Lastly, all the other crimes he had committed: rape, assault, murder, espionage, fraud, treason, it was all there.

The list didn't necessarily scare me I had seen it all before, just maybe not all at the same time with the same person, and not in such a high volume. But that is what I did, this is what I do. I would usually spend hours into the night reading files and preparing meal plans, strict schedules, even rearranging my home if needed. With this I had nothing, nowhere to go. I went to the patient quarters and changed the sheets, got clean towels, and removed any objects that could possibly be used as weapons. Thumbtacks, pencils, even cardboard, then tested all security systems. The house was quiet, empty. I breathed in and decided to celebrate my last bit of alone time by having a good meal, running a bath, and trying to go to bed early.

I sat at the table eating my dinner and reading an article, but I wasn't retaining any of it, just skimming over the words. I felt a high running through me. I finished my dinner, washed my dishes, and headed for that bath. I sat on the edge of the tub while my water filled, dipping my hand to test the temperature. I slipped down into the soapy water and felt the day dissolve off me. The bubbles snapped and popped like champagne fizz all around me. I slowed my breathing, trying to calm my mind and prepare for sleep.

At some point I have to get out, I told myself. The water was starting to cool. I stood and reached for my towel. There is something to be said for a good routine, and I was good at sticking to a routine, it brought order. I washed my face, brushed my teeth, and set my jogging clothes out for the next morning, folded down my covers and crawled into bed, pulling them up to my neck. I closed my eyes and tried to imagine how tomorrow would go. Little did I know then, that tomorrow would change my way of life in ways I would never have believed.

Chapter 2
Captain Miller

My alarm sounded at its normal time, but 5:30 a.m. seemed to come earlier than it normally does. Despite going to bed on time I had tossed and turned all night. I kept being forced awake by nightmares, stupid inconsequential visions jolting me awake. Colonel Weaver and an unknown face coming after me, and to top it off, an onslaught of the regular dream stuff: can't run, can't scream, everyone is against you. I peeled my covers off and willed my body to get up. I sat on the edge of my bed with my head in my hands and listened to my heart beating in my temples. Just then I heard the coffee maker beep and my body decided to cooperate and walk to the kitchen. The coffee routine could be done half-dead, half-asleep was nothing. I made my way to the kitchen, pulling my robe on while I went. I opened the cupboard and examined the many mugs lined up in rows. I picked the big mug this morning, cream and two sugars, and with each sip of coffee I melted into a semi-normal me. I was two sips from normal when my running shoes called for me, taunting me with waves, sand, and fresh air. I rolled my eyes, inhaled deeply and put the coffee cup to my lips thinking very strongly, "Leave me be". But the shoes won this argument.

I headed to the bedroom and dressed; I laced my shoes up with a little more disdain than usual. As I stretched, I caught a glimpse of myself in the mirror. For some reason it intrigued me. Maybe it was the flirtatious nature of Colonel Weaver the day before, but something seemed different. I walked over to the mirror and looked at myself. I was average height, curvy but fit, long blonde hair that had a natural wave. Green eyes, I liked my green eyes, and the freckles that ran across my nose. I had never thought of myself as beautiful, but also not ugly, it's not like I had low self-esteem, I was, just me. I shrugged, not thinking much of the reflection. "It is what it is", I thought.

As I ran, my footsteps seemed hollow, like I was floating just above the ground. Everything seemed so careful and calculated, my body did what it always did but my mind wandered all over the place. I was focused on nothing and everything all at once. At this point, Sid seemed like a lifetime ago and yet like yesterday. My conversation with Colonel Weaver just hours before seemed fake, like it was one of my dreams from that night. Yet my body held this eager energy for what was coming. I was ready. *"You can do this"*. The words kept running through my head. Was I encouraging myself or reassuring myself? Either way it was working. I was pressing on, and I was ready for it.

My legs felt like jelly as I climbed the stairs of my back deck; I knew I'd feel better after a hot shower. Before I could even get there, my stomach lurched. I guess my wandering brain had pushed my body a little harder than I had thought. My ears started ringing and white was closing in, oh no. I ran for the bathroom. Hunched over the toilet I gagged and retched, holding my hair back. I sat there for a few minutes, resting my head on my arm, waiting for the nausea to pass. I stood slowly and stripped down to my bra and underwear, and stared into my closet as if I didn't know what to wear. Rows of suits and skirts, rows of navy heels, and rows of neatly pressed white shirts followed by drawers of nude stockings.

Shower first, then clothes.

I was right, as the hot water ran over me, I could feel it melt away the anxiety of the coming worry, the unknown. I stood there with my hand braced against the wall, the room filled with swirling steam, hot water running off my head and dripping down my body. I watched as it dripped and circled down the drain taking the nausea and worrying with it.

Feeling much better now, I dressed, calmly making sure every piece of my uniform was just right and walked out into the empty foyer. I busied myself with several random and probably pointless tasks, letting my mind focus while I waited. As I paced, the sound of my heels was sharp and deafening on the black marble floors. I caught a glimpse of myself in the entry-way mirror; it wasn't even me I saw. The person looking back at me was uncertain and nervous. When did I lose my edge? I walked over to the mirror, placed both hands in front of me bracing myself on the table and leaned in.

"What is wrong with you?" I asked myself out loud. Just then my self-talk was interrupted by the sound of the gate and the house system notifying me of a visitor. I looked at myself once more, this time I looked more like me, and spoke: "Here we go!"

I stood to attention while several officers came in before Colonel Weaver. This time a more normal, or appropriate, interaction took place between the colonel and me. He saluted, shook my hand and motioned for the other two soldiers, who had stayed stationed at the door, to come in. They held a man, shackled, handcuffed, and blind-folded, under the armpits, and proceeded to drag him in through the door. He wasn't resisting, just not doing anything to help. I almost wondered if he was conscious at all. He was dressed in tattered clothing, feculent and reeking, with tangles of hair and a long, unkempt beard. The blindfold was tied very tightly around his eyes; I could see the skin strained and bulging around it. They stopped a few feet from me and dropped him, almost threw him, to the ground at my feet.

Instinct surely kicked in, I dropped to my knees and started to place my hands on him. A steely voice right behind me said: "Stand. Up. Major Giles." I reluctantly stood and looked Colonel Weaver right in the eyes.

"This man is a war criminal, a murderer, and traitor, he is dangerous and does not deserve your sympathy and surely not your respect."

I fought back many urges in that moment but simply replied with, "Yes, sir".

Colonel Weaver, his hands behind his back, paced in front of me, just a few steps and he would turn and start the pattern over. He mentioned some details that I had already read in the file and finished with, "Your objective, Major, is to get what is in his head out of his mouth. Keep me posted on anything that he tells you..." He paused, briefly stopping in front of me, looked me square in the eyes and finished: "Anything he tells you, Major, and feel free to let me know of any other 'breakthroughs'. He used hand quotation marks when he said the word breakthroughs. He was mocking me, mocking psychology. He motioned for the soldiers to move out, only to turn to me and say, "Oh and Major, he is only rushing off to his death, so time is not really of the essence. Be thorough, take your time with this one." Our "normal" meeting had suddenly shifted with the return of the slimy smile and a wink.

He followed the last soldier out, glancing back at the prisoner on the floor. I could not read the emotion on his face, but it sent chills running down my spine. The door closed behind him, and I heard the tires on the driveway as the procession of military vehicles left me there with this crumpled man on the floor.

In an instant I felt so many emotions run through me, I just had to land on one to cultivate. I thought quickly about his file and the list of offenses, and the brief description of his childhood. In the past I have learned that in order to get respect, you have to give respect. That is not always a practice used in the military, but I was, first and foremost, a doctor.

Slowly, I knelt beside him. He reminded me of a

wounded animal, lying helpless, bound in the fetal position. I felt this strange pulling of two urges, usually known as fight or flight, because while wounded animals can be vulnerable, they can also be very dangerous. I thought to coddle him like a mother with, "Everything is going to be okay." I also considered just walking away. I can't really say I was, or wasn't, expecting what came out of my mouth in that moment.

"I am not going to hurt you," I said, quietly and calmly.

The truth was, if he left me no choice, I most certainly would hurt him, but I knew if a person doesn't feel safe there is no progress, so I lied.

"I am going to remove this blindfold, okay?" I said, reaching for the dirty knot at the back of his head.

There was no answer, but he didn't move. The knot was so tight I couldn't manage to get it off, every time I tried to untie the knot, he would wince away from me.

"I will be right back, okay." I said, feeling like a play-by-play might be best.

As I walked away, I was glad that his smell was not wafting up my nose. I also found myself feeling very bad for him being in that condition. I went to my office and got my medical scissors; I took several deep breaths of the fresh air to prepare myself for minimal, shallow breaths again. I slid the scissors right behind his ear under the bandage and cut. Instantly, his already closed eyes clenched tightly shut, and he flinched away. He had been in darkness for some time, I realized, and the light was too much.

"*Dim the lights,*" I said loudly.

The house complied, and the lights dimmed. Still lying on his side on the floor he lifted his head a bit, blinked several times and looked at me. Though it only lasted a fraction of a second the moment our eyes met my ears started ringing, not like the ringing before something bad happens but like the whooshing of air all around you begging for your attention, and there in that moment, however small, I felt safe with him.

His head fell to the side, slumped onto his shoulder like he had exhausted all his energy just by lifting it for that moment. I scrambled to unlock the shackles around his ankles. I had to wiggle the key a few times to get the lock to release. There was a red, inflamed, scabbed-over band that circled around each ankle, it was the same around his wrists under the handcuffs. I slid my hand under his arm.

"Alright, Captain, we are going to get up now, can you help me at all?"

He proceeded to roll a bit to one side, first getting on one knee, and with a big heave, I helped him to his feet. I stepped back to be able to take him all in, but not too far in case he decided to go down again. He stretched his back out like a cat in the sun. It almost seemed involuntary, as though standing upright was the best feeling in the world.

"Well, Captain Miller, there is no polite way to put this, you are a mess. So, first things first." I motioned with my head for him to follow me.

After taking the first step, he stumbled and I rushed to help him, but with a hand braced on his knee, he held up the other hand as though to tell me that he could do it. I was grateful because I wasn't sure I could manage to help him and not gag at the odor emanating from him. I started to walk more slowly down the hall, I felt his presence behind me as I walked. I counted to myself the number of steps to his bathroom, "Eighteen, nineteen, twenty." I stood to the side and motioned toward the door. "There is a clean towel on the vanity and whatever else you need will be in the cupboard behind the door."

He seemed to hesitate as he walked slowly through the doorway, his eyes darting every which way. He seemed like an animal that didn't want to get into a crate. I resisted the urge to put my foot on his back-side and push him through the door.

Maybe rushing a bit, I grabbed the door handle and quickly shut the door behind him. As soon as the door was between us emotions bubbled up inside me. I am not sure how long I stood with my back to the door, three minutes, maybe four, until the door was flung open. I jumped slightly and turned, stunned to see Captain Miller, naked with his arms held out to his sides. I blushed and quickly turned my back to him.

"Captain Miller, there is no need for inspection." I fought the urge to giggle. "Please take your time, wash, relax, whatever else you might need. There is shampoo and body wash in the cabinet, left is hot, and right is cold"

I kept my back to him, although I couldn't help but wonder what his face looked like. Was he embarrassed too? I covered my smile with my hand.

"I don't see saving your hair at this point, give it a good wash and I'll give it a healthy cut, the beard too." I sort of turned to gesture which direction to look. "And there is fresh clothing and a toothbrush in the cupboard behind the door, throw the old ones in the garbage next to the sink. Take your time. I will be out here when you are dressed and ready."

I proceeded to walk away, my pace quickening with each step, then I heard the door close. I sat on my couch to wait. As a doctor, I was used to seeing nudity, it was part of the job. So why was I blushing? Twenty minutes went by, then thirty. I was almost getting concerned when the door opened followed by a billow of steam. I stood as Captain Miller came out wearing white scrubs that hung on his body; he held a wad of his pants in his hand, clearly holding them up.

I was able to get a better view of the man that had been thrown at my feet a crumpled mess. Captain Miller was tall, probably 6'2" maybe 6'3", he was emaciated, his skin hung off his bones, but you could see the memory of muscle there. His eyes were a piercing pale blue, and he had full lips, though it was hard to say what he truly looked like because his facial features were sunken in, dark circles firmly planted under his eyes. He had dark hair that was knotted everywhere. We stood there looking at each other, I am sure he could feel my eyes taking him in.

"Much better," I said. "Now come with me, let's get a good look at you, and handle that hair."

I led him downstairs to my examination room, where there was a white tile floor with white file cabinets and white shelving lining the walls. A dark mahogany desk sat in the corner. As I entered the room, I realized how institutional it was, cold and unwelcoming. Why had I not put any plant life in here? There was an examination table in the center of the room covered in that thin, noisy paper. I motioned for him to sit. The lights were bright, and he still seemed sensitive, so that's where I started. I took my ophthalmoscope, leaned in close, and peered into his eyes. My stomach fluttered and his eyes shifted and looked straight into mine, it was like he knew, as if he could hear the change in my heart rate or that he felt my stomach flutter at the closeness to him.

I cleared my throat. "There doesn't seem to be any lasting damage in your eyes, Captain Miller. I would assume that your light sensitivity will wear off soon, but I have some eye drops that might help."

I continued my examination, administered vitamins and antibiotics, listened, and observed. During the examination I noticed he had many scars, on his arms, his neck and shoulders, and many on his back, lashing marks. I couldn't help it, I reached out to touch the marks on his back, tracing along the scars with varying degrees of healing. I looked up at him only to find that he was looking at me, curiosity written all over his face. I stopped quickly and walked over to a chair that sat next to the desk in the corner. He didn't seem to say much with his voice, but his face betrayed his every thought.

"Come sit over here, Captain, let's take care of that hair. I am afraid it all has to go; I hope you aren't too attached." Silently, he stood and complied. I noticed he was still holding his pants in a wad at his waistband. "Oh, here, let me show you how to work this thing." I lifted his shirt to find the tab that tightened the waistband. He flinched slightly; I thought I had hurt him but realized quickly that I hadn't. "Ticklish I see," I joked. He didn't seem amused, so I moved on.

I stood behind him with my clippers, taking section after section, while his dark hair fell to his shoulders and then to the floor. I walked around to face him, and began shaving his beard, with each stroke I started to see him. I held him under his chin, his beard now a short stubble, a five o'clock shadow.

"There you are!" I said, with a small smile.

I could tell now that he had a very strong jawline, and a broad nose slightly crooked at the bridge, not because he was born that way but like he had broken it a time or two, there was still some swelling, and I knew it was recently. His lips were full and very well-shaped. Our eyes locked briefly, his gaze spoke a thousand words, I felt them, but I could not discern them. I knew then what challenge lay before me; I wasn't really one to walk away from a challenge, especially when I knew I had the tools to win.

I was energized, I felt like there was electricity dancing in the air, fueling my every move.

"Let's fatten you up," I said cheerfully, walking to the kitchen. I was reminded of a puppy bouncing after their owner to the food bowl and I smiled to myself. "Please have a seat, Captain, do you mind if I call you William?" And still he said nothing. "Okay, Captain it is." I found myself glancing over my shoulder to see if he was there. He was standing at the window that overlooked the beach, his arms crossed behind his back. He was so gaunt; I could tell his diet was the kind strictly to keep alive and not to nourish in any way. I would have to start slow, or he would just end up vomiting everything up.

Day one: oatmeal with applesauce and milk. I asked him to join me, he sat, we ate, no one spoke. I started to say something a few times then thought better of it, which created an all-new awkward silence. I expected Captain Miller to devour his food in one bite, but he managed to maintain table manners. Now if I could get him to maintain pleasant conversation we could get somewhere. I couldn't complain, Captain Miller did as I asked without complaint or hesitation between questions and paperwork. Otherwise, he was there standing with his arms crossed behind his back, staring out the window.

The morning went on in silence, I had thought to come up with my own plan in silence. I busied myself in psychology books, although I found myself staring at the page and not reading anything, followed by reading the same sentence seventeen times and not retaining a single word. Luckily, my stomach growled and reminded me I had something to do other than sit there and wonder what to do, or say, to this man who had taken up residency in my house, and who was more like a stray cat than a human being.

"Captain Miller?" I said. No answer.

"Captain?" I asked again, a bit louder. I could tell I had pulled him out of somewhere deep in his mind. He turned and there was sadness on his face. Not just bad-day sadness but intense sorrow. It pulled at my heartstrings. I wanted to hold him, to comfort him. I had to shrug it off, file it somewhere in my head and try to use it to my advantage. "Have a seat, Captain, let's eat some lunch."

We ate in silence once more, the awkwardness still thick and looming, this time accompanied by lingering unspoken questions. As I cut my meat, I daydreamed about jumping on the table and screaming just to break the silence. I pictured what reaction Captain Miller would have to such a thing, and a giggle slipped out. I cleared my throat to try and hide it."

"So..." I trailed off, trying to hide the small smile on my face. Just then he stood up, shooting me a strange look. I assumed it was because of my random laughter. He made eye contact briefly then looked away. He took his tray to the sink, rinsed it off then returned to the window with his back to me. I was still standing, perplexed, by the table, holding my empty food tray.

"Not one for small talk," I muttered under my breath in a snarky tone, and then his breathing changed. If it hadn't been for the extreme silence I had grown used to, I wouldn't have noticed. I looked up and I swear, if you could tell by the back of someone's head, he was smiling.

I knew, this being day one, that we wouldn't get anywhere. Colonel Weaver had one thing right, this was going to take some time. I had time, I was patient. I sat back down at the table and watched him from behind. Maybe I had something with the stray cat theory. Small triumphs would be my fuel here, there was no room for big breakthroughs yet. I stood up again and stepped closer to him.

"Captain Miller, you must be tired, you are welcome to come sit with me." I picked up a book and headed toward the sofa. With no response, I left him to his devices and went about my day. I tried to read again with the same result as before. I instead busied myself with everyday activities, and at times I forgot I wasn't alone as I found myself talking to my plants or humming a tune while I flitted around the house. This was strange to me because it meant I felt comfortable, I wasn't supposed to feel comfortable with this man, this treasonous murderer. I suppose it was because I had convinced myself that he was a cat instead. My thought process took me to my examination, his eyes. There was kindness there, as another William said it, "The eyes are the window into the soul." I would take that; I could build on that.

Surprisingly, the day had flown by. We had sat together for two meals and were about to sit for a third, and still Captain Miller hadn't spoken any words to me, not a single word. So, once I got dinner cooking, I thought it was time to show the captain the ropes around here. I walked up to him; he didn't look or move but an acknowledgment passed in the space between us.

"Come with me," was all I said, somehow knowing he would follow. I thought it a little cocky, but it seemed I was getting good at reading his body language, if you can call it that. I could tell when he was with me, and when he was somewhere else entirely.

The next few minutes I felt like an amusement park guide, this is this, that is that. "If you would look to your left," sort of thing. I showed him everything he needed to find and everything that was restricted. I went over his schedule and how things would work. I ran a tight ship complete with daily chores and often-times long sessions. The expression on his face seemed blank, with a touch of pleased, the entire time. I was baffled by him, and because of that I was thoroughly intrigued and drawn to him. Although it seemed like I could read him, I couldn't be sure I was being accurate. He was, of course, a highly trained special forces soldier, trained to withstand torture and pass lie detector tests, all tells erased.

During dinner we sat across from each other, this time in a comfortable silence, like two old roommates who didn't need to fill every moment with meaningless conversation. I was flipping through an old medical magazine article about genes versus environment when I felt his gaze shift, and as I met his glance, he absorbed all of me. His alluring blue eyes held me, again it was like they were speaking out loud to me, but I had to learn the language. His broad and slightly crooked nose breathed me into him and his full lips, though never moving, I knew had so much to say. He held my gaze for moments, seconds really. I let out my breath a little too quickly and then noticed I had been holding it. There it was again, only for a small juncture in time, the non-smile. I think most people wouldn't have noticed it, but I did, and couldn't stop myself from smiling back. I felt my cheeks flush with heat and quickly dropped my gaze back to my article.

I cleared my throat awkwardly and stood up. "Well, Captain, I daresay we just had our first conversation." I nodded politely, took his plate and turned to the kitchen.

"I will take care of the dishes tonight; you may go get accustomed to your new room."

Then, for the first time that day, he disobeyed me. He came and stood next to me at the sink and started washing. I gladly followed suit mainly because I hated doing dishes, but also because for some reason I enjoyed his company. I grabbed the towel and dried every dish he handed me. He was good, and I was picky. After the dishes were done, he proceeded to wipe down counters and sweep the floor while I prepped breakfast for the next morning. I was bewildered at how quickly I fell into sync with Captain Miller, how quickly I felt safe around him, but there was that logical person there screaming silently to beware, be careful, be smart. "I know, I've got this," I told my inner self. "He's just a cat after all," I joked, then quickly found myself hoping he wasn't a mind reader.

After everything was cleaned and put away, I took Captain Miller back to his room. It was a small room with a single bed, a small dresser, and a desk.

"Here it is, it's not the Hilton, but it will do." I gestured to the bed. He walked slowly into the room and sat on the bed running his hand on the mattress, then stopped at the pillow and picked it up, almost hugging it to his chest. Something told me he hadn't had a mattress, or a pillow, in some time. Wait until he sees the blanket, I thought jokingly.

"Well, good night," I said awkwardly and unable to hide my internal joking from my voice. He looked up at me. My heart fluttered in my chest and with every ounce of my being I felt 'thank you' emanating from him. I cleared my throat again trying to right myself before I spoke this time. "If you need an extra blanket, or anything else, let me know."

I walked out of the room and pulled the door behind me. The door closed with a bang, and I suddenly felt cold. I placed my hand on the scanner outside his door and it locked, echoing down the hall. The light changed from green to glowing red. I walked the few steps down the hall to my bedroom to lock down the rest of the house from the control panel on my wall. And now, in full circle, here I was again, lying quietly in my bed staring at the control panel lights, all red. The place was locked down, the wind blew softly through my curtains, and they danced to the tune of the waves crashing outside. My breathing seemed to harmonize, and I fell into the deepest sleep.

Chapter 3
Ailments

I expected my daily reports of "No change" to Colonel Weaver would spark somewhat of a red flag and he would show up, guns blazing, but weeks had passed and there was silence on his end. I honestly wasn't sure to be concerned or relieved. Maybe both. It had seemed as though what Captain Miller had to say was of the utmost importance, so I found it hard to understand that he had bigger fish to fry. I wasn't really wanting to see him, or deal with it, so I pushed it to the back of my mind. I wasn't superstitious much, but I feared if I thought about it, he would come.

The days were all about the same. I talked; Captain Miller listened. He followed all the rules perfectly, my own and those of the military. He was to be clean shaven and wear his government-assigned clothing, he was considered dangerous, therefore he wore all white. To break any of the rules given by me or them would result in punishment, usually in the form of lashings. Living with Captain Miller was like living in a silent movie, unfortunately for me there was no background music. In most cases you would think life to be dull, but I had grown used to his presence, it was comforting. I had decided that it was more like living with a dog than a cat. Cats were independent and had an attitude. Captain Miller was definitely more dog-like, a silent companion that offers an amount of loyalty that you don't fully understand.

I was seated at the breakfast table, waiting for Captain Miller to join me. The bathroom door opened and I looked up. He stood tall in the doorway, beads of water still on his head and neck. He filled out his clothing now and had a healthy glow. He had opted to keep his close haircut, and it suited him. I could see the outline of his muscles through his shirt. He was my living GQ magazine I had all to myself. I couldn't help feeling that way, he really was glorious to look at.

"Alright, Captain," I said, rubbing my hands together in fabricated glee. "Let's have our session!"

I could often tell how Captain Miller was feeling based purely on his eyes, but today he was not amused by my silly antics. It had gotten fairly easy to shrug it off, what had to be done had to be done, and if nothing changes, nothing changes.

He hurried through his paperwork today, scribbly check marks instead of neatly filling in the circles. Puzzled, I started to ask, "Are you feeling alright today?" I trailed off, knowing he wouldn't answer and pretended to shift through some paperwork.

Captain Miller sat at the breakfast table, but he seemed to be moving his food around his plate more than he was eating it. I had become annoyed by the difference in his attitude today. Why was I annoyed? It was my job to pick him apart, I should be excited at a change in attitude, it meant that something was different. So, instead of making meaningless one-sided conversation, I wrapped up inside my brain and waited there. When I came back around to reality, I had finished eating, yet had tasted nothing. Once my mind came back into focus, I saw that Captain Miller was no longer sitting there. When had he gone, and why didn't I notice? It was just his full plate and empty space staring at me. Was I so wrapped up that I had completely lost myself. How long was I gone? How long was *he* gone? A small panic ran down my spine. I stood quickly and thought to look in his quarters first.

I walked quickly to his room, though it seemed like slow motion. Once I got to the door, I saw Captain Miller lying in his bed, his arms and legs pulled into himself in the fetal position. I rushed to his side, asking all sorts of unanswered questions. As soon as I got close enough to touch him, I felt the heat radiating off him, I put my hand to his head. He was burning up, yet his hands and feet were like ice. I ran to get my medical kit. I was nervous and scared but I knew I was trained for this, I got my mind right, and my hands steady. His temperature was 104.6, that was my first task. I injected a fever reducer into his hip then waited, the ticking of my watch was loud in my ears, the rushing of air in and out of my lungs was enough to drive me crazy. I tried to examine what I could to find a culprit, a rash, or something to tell me what was causing this. I took his temperature again. 104.8.

"We can't wait," I said. "Come on, Captain, let's go."

He groaned as I tried to pry his arms away from him and help him up. In all of the craziness I felt a zing because that was the first time I had ever heard his voice. A sting of tears behind my eyes drove me on.

"I can't do this without your help, William, come on, help me."

One more tug and he was off the bed, struggling to stand. The weight of him was considerable because he couldn't help much, but we made our way limping along to the bathroom, his arm draped over me. I stripped him down and he shivered uncontrollably. He was really going to hate what I was about to do. I turned on the shower and all but pushed him in. He fell to his knees, his body arched and writhed, looking grotesque, because the water was freezing. I shrank back and watched while his body adapted to the temperature, eventually the shivering was almost gone. While I had always believed in God, I had never spent too much time talking with him, but today I closed my eyes and prayed.

I turned off the water and knelt to help Captain Miller up. Our eyes met and I knew that he was grateful, and I knew that he knew I was scared. That fear, any uneasiness I might have felt during all of this, could attest to an abundance of emotions, but they all pointed to one thing, affection. I had an irrefutable adoration for Captain Miller.

We tried to make our way back to his room, but he

began to stumble. My room was closer, so I turned to go in. I could feel him fighting against me.

"It's okay," I whispered.

We limped together slowly to my bed, his weight getting more and more heavy, and I could feel his body heating up again. He fell onto my bed in one awkward lump and the shivering started again. The doctor in me had kicked in, full throttle. I was afraid I was going to have to save his life, and I found myself grateful for the knowledge to do so. I left him and ran to my medical room, once there, instinct took over. I opened cupboards and drawers, grabbing things at will. My brain had pushed emotion aside and taken over. When I got back, he was unresponsive. My hands were working as my mind prioritized every symptom in a mental to-do list.

Time passed in a strange sort of sped-up standing still. I sat next to the bed watching the air come in and out of his lungs, listening to the sound of his heart monitor beeping. I had run an IV and given him everything I could to make him comfortable. The fever was still there but holding steady at 103.8. I sat, I watched, I researched, sleep was coming, my fight to stay awake was growing weaker until sleep finally won.

A bright light woke me. I was lying down. I blinked several times to clear my eyes. I wasn't home anymore; I was me, I mean I felt like me. I was dressed all in white, in a knee-length dress. The material was stiff and unflattering. I stood taking in my surroundings, an infinite white room, the light fading into the distance. There was nothing. I was unable to tell if there was no sound or if I couldn't hear, it seemed like a thick fuzziness clinging around me. Every move I made seemed labored, no that's not right. Slow, reluctant, somehow. I suddenly felt someone approach me from behind, a feeling of dread, the feeling that I should run.

Confused and disoriented I stood still and waited, I had nowhere to go, I was going have to face my attacker head on. I could feel the warmth of a body standing behind me, I turned my head slightly to see. There was nothing. Suddenly, I flinched at the distinct feeling of hot breath whispering in my ear, there were no words, only the breath and the thoughts running through my mind, as though I was reading subtitles in a foreign film where you spend all your time reading and miss the movie entirely.

The fuzz ended abruptly with my ears ringing and I knew I could hear again, even though there was no sound, the clarity was there. I turned around quickly, ready to fight. There was no one there, just the infinite white room. Then there it was, sound in the distance, but which way? I started to run, the heaviness of my body began breaking down and falling away as though I was wrapped in some sort of cocoon. Faster and faster until suddenly the sound was right there.

"Major Giles?"

"*Major. Wake up!*"

I jolted awake, sleep still lingering on my face. I was alone, sitting in the chair next to my bed. I must have been dreaming. How long had I been asleep? What time was it? Suddenly the questions stopped, and my heart jumped. Where was Captain Miller? My bed was disheveled, the IV lying there, all proof that I was in fact no longer dreaming. I looked at the control panel: green. The entire house was unlocked, I jumped out of the chair, frantic, and headed toward the door. I stopped suddenly. I saw him standing, as he always did, staring out the window. This time, however, as I stood in the hallway he looked at me, and our eyes met. My mind reeled. I remembered my dream again, a man standing behind me, but this time I could see and hear him clearly, it was Colonel Weaver, he was whispering in my ear: "I am coming for you."

My mind had blocked it out in the dream, but now it was all clear, which was scary and confusing. Then I was back staring eye to eye with Captain Miller, a thousand emotions written on his face: fear, adoration, and gratitude. I quickly walked over to him and pressed the back of my hand to his head. It was dry and cool. I couldn't find it in me to remain professional, I leaned my forehead on his shoulder and whispered, "You had me scared there, soldier."

The sentence floated around the room, echoing off the walls, and lingered in our minds. I stood there next to him in a one-sided embrace, and time stood still.

Captain Miller, my silent partner, and I had our routine down, we had our roles and we played them well. Today, however, I asked several unanswered questions and flitted around him like a terminally ill patient in a hospice ward. His face was always reading, "I'm fine," but I could feel his weakness, I knew. We had won the battle, but the war was still raging inside him. I had tried several anti-viral's, but which one had worked? Were we out of the woods?

Why wouldn't he just lie down and get better? Why was he pushing himself? I finally got him to at least sit, and I handed him his paperwork.

As he sat there, staring down at the paper, the door suddenly flew open. I jumped; the house hadn't warned us that someone had entered the gate.

Colonel Weaver strutted through the door. As he stepped over the threshold, he removed his sunglasses and gave me a menacing look. I expected him to greet me, but he went straight to the table where Captain Miller was sitting.

"Mr. Miller," he boomed with a cold voice. "My, my, look at you, this seems almost inhumane."

Speechless, I trailed after him.

He put his hand on the back of Captain Miller's neck. Weak and tired as Miller was, I saw the muscles strain in his face as he tried to fight against Colonel Weaver.

"Colonel, I wasn't expecting you..." I trailed off as he lifted his hand; he was telling me to shut up. He bent down and put his lips to Captain Miller's ear. I could not hear him, but I would swear I saw him mouth the words, "I am coming for you."

He stopped his assault on Captain Miller and motioned with his finger for me to follow him. I became aware that I was disheveled and messy after sleeping in the chair next to my bed. I feared what was about to happen between Colonel Weaver and myself. He turned the corner into my bedroom and my heart skipped a beat, but I followed him. He was looking around the room, taking it all in, but I could not read his face. My bed was unmade and there was an IV stationed next to it, and medical equipment strewn across my end table and dresser.

He whipped around and we were face-to-face. His quick movement made me jump back, but he grabbed my wrist, bending my arm up by my face and pushing me against the wall. I didn't have time to react before he leaned in close and smelled my neck, deeply and purposefully. I fought the urge to cringe at his closeness. He reached up and snatched my hair clip out of my hair sending my hair sprawling out over my shoulders and down my back. He took a lock of hair between his fingers and rubbed it between his lips. All politeness and properness had left me, and I snapped.

"What do you want, Weaver?" Acid seeped through every word.

Before I could even get a breath, his hand was around my throat, he was squeezing tight, so tight. My hands pulled at his fingers trying too free myself from his grasp, but he was far too strong. Panic was setting in, surely, he didn't intend to kill me. He released one hand from my throat and began brushing the stray hairs from my face.

"There, that's better," he said, still holding my throat. "You forget your place, Presley." The sound of my name coming out of his mouth made me nauseated. "I will let it slide since we have a date tomorrow. I wouldn't want to go and ruin it with a crushed windpipe." With one last squeeze he released me, and I fell coughing to the floor, holding my neck. I stared up at my attacker, shocked and confused, and I knew it was written all over my face. He stared back at me, like he pitied me. Then it shifted to something menacing and disgusting.

"Wear something ... nice. Be ready by six," he said, and left the room. He left me there on the floor. I didn't move until I heard the front gate close. I quickly tried to gather my wits and my breath. My legs shook under me, but I managed to stand. Slowly, I walked out to the corridor where Captain Miller sat at the table, his head hung in defeat. For the first time since he had arrived in my home I felt anger toward him, anger for making me feel anything for him, anger for abandoning me when I needed him. For the time being rational thought was gone and only fear was left. I turned and walked back into my room, shut the door and walked to my control panel, and switched it to LOCK. I didn't come out for the rest of the day, and I didn't care.

Chapter 4
The Date

The sun pierced through the window and drilled into my eyes. I had to have fallen asleep at some point last night having been rudely awakened by this laser boring into my brain. As soon as my eyes opened my head split and pounded. Interesting that mornings are so conveniently a result of the night. Then, like a fire alarm in my mind, I remembered I had left Captain Miller sitting at the table yesterday after Colonel Weaver had left. Okay, okay, it wasn't fair to blame him for anything, but I needed a scapegoat and it happened to be him. The beeping of my coffee machine brought me back; I inhaled the beautiful coffee smell wafting into my room. I dressed quickly, if only to get to the coffee. I opened my bedroom door and, oh my gosh! I jumped back two feet and put my hand on my chest, my heart pounding.

"Captain, you scared the life out of me!"

He was just standing there, right outside my door. His gaze was intense, but he had dark circles under his eyes and beads of sweat glistening on his forehead.

"Captain Miller," I said sternly, "you are not well, get back to your quarters, I will bring your breakfast to your room this morning." The look on his face shifted. I guess when you don't speak your other expressions intensify because I suddenly knew that he was relieved that I wasn't mad at him anymore. For an instant I saw something in his eyes, his expression softened, it was gratitude, then to my surprise he turned and went back to his room. Maybe I was wearing down the stubborn soldier in him.

As I stood in the kitchen making breakfast, I remembered the last events of the day before. My vision blanked out, I wasn't seeing what was in front of me anymore, it was like a dream, a nightmare. One thing was for sure, I had to go on this date, I didn't know what Colonel Weaver was capable of. I wanted to believe that people are mostly good and that they aren't evil, only misguided, but I had seen a lot of ugliness in the human race. I could only imagine the worst and hope for the best.

I gathered a tray of food and walked down the hall to Captain Miller's room. When I got there, he was lying on his side facing away from me. I thought for a moment that he was asleep, but his breathing was too shallow. I wondered if Captain Miller would try and stop me. I wondered to what lengths he would go. His hatred for Colonel Weaver was a given, I wouldn't need him to tell me that, but what did he care about my well-being?

"I have your breakfast, Captain." My voice shaky and

unsure, he turned to look at me. I slid the tray on the desk and quicky grabbed hold of the door. Grateful that the captain was sick, because I believed that was the only reason I was quicker than him. I backed out and the door slammed shut before he got to his feet. He pressed his face up to the small window in the door and our eyes met. We stared, wide-eyed, as I backed away slowly. I knew that going with Colonel Weaver was something I had to do, but I didn't know what Captain Miller would or wouldn't do, and I had to make sure my plans were on my terms. We stared a moment through the glass. I could tell by his gaze he was trying to portray his feelings and I tried to do the same back. I knew of all people in this world, Captain Miller might be one who knows more about what Colonel Weaver is capable of. When I finally turned my back to him and walked away, one thought was prominent: he doesn't want me to go with Colonel Weaver, and if he doesn't want me to go, it can only be because he cares.

It was late morning, and I had the entire day to get ready for the so-called date. I probably could have used Captain Miller's company to occupy my brain and keep me from anxiety. Instead, I opted to go for a run. I took my time on this run, took in all the scenery and as much fresh air as my lungs could take. I stopped at the lighthouse and sat on a rock. A horn from a barge passing by sounded in the distance. I had never really dated much out of high school, let alone with a man who seemed like a narcissistic sociopath. I was starting to feel guilty for what I had done to Captain Miller, maybe my run home would wise me back up.

Shortly after I got home, I could hear a sound coming from Captain Miller's room. I walked down the hall and pressed my ear to his door to hear it clearly. He was tapping, tap, tap, tap. I pushed it from my mind and tried to go about my day, but the cadence of it was getting stuck in my mind. It didn't take long to realize it was repeating a rhythm over and over. It seemed familiar, a song, a beat. I couldn't put my finger on it and tried harder to ignore it. Tap, tap, tap.

As the day wore on, I got nervous, nauseated, and my palms were sweaty. Every sound echoed through my skull: the clock ticking, Captain Miller tapping; tick, tock, tap, tap. I thought I might go mad. With the clock reminding me that time was racing on, and Captain Miller reminding me that he was not giving up, I had a sense of foreboding for what was to come. I flipped on the light to my closet and pushed the suits aside to the very back. I had one dress that I had worn to my mother's funeral; it was a knee-length, black lace, A-line dress, sleeveless with a high neck. It would have to do.

I stood in the foyer of my house, dressed in black, with my hair up in a French twist, a few curls cascading down. I had put on the pearl earrings my mother left to me and I tightly held my black clutch purse. I am not sure what happened first, the realization that I could hear the gate or the familiarity of Captain Miller's tapping.

-.. --- -. .----. - / --. ---

And with that, I jumped, startled at the knocking on my door. My cheeks were flushed with heat, I reluctantly opened the door.

Colonel Weaver stood in the light of my porch, arm braced on the entryway, feet crossed in front of him, looking down at his free hand like he was making sure there were still five fingers there. Slowly, he glanced up at me, stepped back and looked me up and down approvingly. As much as I hated to admit it, my heart skipped a beat; he was so handsome, and I had only ever seen him out of uniform once before. He wore black slacks with a silverish button-up shirt, but the top few buttons were left undone and I could see the line of his pectoral muscles showing from the top of his shirt. The sleeves were rolled up and the veins in his muscular arms were showing as though he had just been working out.

"Well, don't just stand there, gorgeous, let's go."

He put his hand on the small of my back and ushered me out to his car. It was a vintage Audi convertible, silver like his shirt, with black leather interior. He started to open the door for me, but as I grabbed it to get in, he stopped me suddenly and got very close. He raised his hand to my face, and I flinched. He then slowly brushed a stray curl from my brow and tucked it behind my ear.

"About the other day." His face twisted in faux disgust. "Let's not let one bad day ruin the evening." He then leaned slightly back and his eyes searched my body. I blinked heavily to hide whatever feeling had just bubbled up inside me and forced a smile. I slid into the car just as Colonel Weaver, using one hand on the window, jumped over his door and landed perfectly in his seat. He looked at me and flashed a huge, straight white smile. "Seatbelts!" he said.

As we sped down my driveway, I heard Captain Miller's tapped cadence in my head. It had just come to me why it was so familiar; it was Morse code. We had taken many classes on it; we still used it sometimes to pass secret messages to soldiers. Over and over again he tapped it, he was saying, "don't go." I closed my eyes and tried to block the tears from escaping.

We drove around the small island for about five minutes. I had seen the building before but had never been inside. It appeared to be some sort of resort, or hotel. We pulled into the parking lot and were met by a young Latino boy in a tuxedo. I thought he was maybe seventeen or eighteen. His hair was a little too long and a curl escaped and tickled his forehead; he kept trying to brush it back into place, to no avail. He opened my door and ushered me to stand next to Colonel Weaver, who shook his hand, casually giving him a tip with a wink. He was acting sly, like James Bond. But to me it came across as more cheesy than debonair.

Once we got inside, I took it all in, looking around the huge square room. The center was littered with tables; all four walls, three stories up, were lined with huge stone columns with beautiful cast-iron railings linking them together. The walls and floor were heavily decorated in colorful Mexican tiles, and tropical plants cascaded from every surface. In the corner of the room a band was playing salsa music. Everywhere I looked people were laughing, eating, and dancing. It was very loud, but pleasant. I noticed a beautiful Latina girl leaning in close to Colonel Weaver. He whispered something into her ear while slipping her a tip as well. She gestured for us to follow.

She took us to a darkened part of the restaurant, through some thick, red velvet curtains and down a stone staircase. At the bottom, in a dimly lit room, were seven or eight tables with white linen tablecloths and three lit candles in the center of each table. There was classical music playing from speakers around the room. She led us to a table and pulled out a chair for me, politely saying, "Javier will be right with you."

There were two other couples seated in the room, one couple was leaning across the table holding hands, the other looked as though it might be on a first date. Just as Colonel Weaver was scooting in his chair, a man came to the table, who I assumed was Javier. He was dressed in a tuxedo, like the boy out front, and had a white towel draped over one arm and another wrapped around a bottle of wine. I didn't drink but didn't want to be rude; I figured I could take little sips throughout dinner. Javier communicated quietly with Colonel Weaver. I strained to hear, but before I could tell what was being said Javier left, leaving me alone with Colonel Weaver. He reached across the table and took my hand. I fought the urge to pull away.

"You look beautiful tonight. Did I fail to tell you that?"

I smiled, somewhat unwillingly, trying so hard to be something like normal. But I couldn't get any words out, just an awkward disapproving smile. As he was about to say something else to me, a tall, slender man in a white suit and hat walked up and whispered in his ear. Without saying anything to me, he stood and followed the man. The restaurant was so dimly lit I didn't get a chance to see who this was or what he looked like aside from his attire. I thought it was possible it was one of the soldiers I had seen Weaver with when he came to bring Captain Miller, but you get so used to seeing everyone in uniform that when they are in their street clothes, they seem like different people altogether.

I sat there alone, rubbing my arms in discomfort for a few minutes, when the waiter arrived with our food. Weaver had ordered for me, I obviously didn't do well to hide the disgust from my face when Javier asked, "Is everything okay, miss?" I managed to give him a believable smile and answer politely: "Yes, thank you, but what is this?"

He bowed his head to me graciously and replied, "Acociles." Then he motioned to the ramekin making a dipping motion and rubbed his stomach in a circular motion. It was far too amusing to watch him than let him know that I spoke Spanish fairly well.

Surprisingly enough, they were good, kind of like shrimp. I ate my dinner alone; it seemed ridiculous to eat them cold. I was tempted to eat Colonel Weaver's too. Where was he? Javier returned and took my empty bowl, and Colonel Weaver's bowl as well, without saying anything to me. He seemed in a hurry. I was drumming my nails on the white tablecloth, and glanced at my arm as though I was wearing a watch, when Colonel Weaver finally walked through the curtain hanging over the doorway. He looked flushed and upset. I straightened my back as he approached.

"Let's go," he said shortly and walked over to my chair to pull it out for me. I stood quickly and started toward the door when he grabbed my arm. "This way." He headed toward a hallway at the back of the restaurant. It was dark, and unnerving, at one point I couldn't see him in front of me and I reached out to find something when I felt him take my hand. He opened the door, there were lantern lights lining the walkway twinkling in the night, the sun had dipped under the horizon, the sky only had a small remnant of the sun's light.

Colonel Weaver led me toward some tall grass down from the back door we had just exited. When we got beyond the grass I saw a blanket, two wine glasses, and a bottle of wine. My footing hesitated but he pushed me forward.

"Have a seat, Major." He still had a hold of my hand and was guiding me to the blanket. "Can we dispense with all the Major this, Major that, Presley?" I hated hearing my name come out of his mouth. I hated this situation; I hated this night. Reluctantly, I sat down. Just as I turned to say something, Colonel Weaver's face was coming toward me. I thought he was going in for a kiss when suddenly he slammed his head right into my temple, full force.

My head ringing, all I could see was black, then white. Before I could even see, I realized that my dress was being removed.

"No!" I tried to yell. Nothing came out. My arms felt like they weighed a thousand pounds, I couldn't move my legs. Pain, the pain, my head was pounding. I was aware of what was going on, but couldn't stop it, I couldn't focus on anything, my head turned slowly from side to side like my body was trying to expel the pain. I felt my legs being pushed apart, I lay there half naked, and cold, and I tried to resist. Hot tears ran down my face and dripped in my ears and in my hair. I closed my eyes.

Colonel Weaver was on top of me, his body wedged between my legs. With every breath I felt strength coming back to me, every heartbeat was driving me forward now. I was a fool to think he wouldn't notice my senses coming back. I felt an ice-cold blade against my throat, followed by his hot breath, so sure and confident.

"This is happening," he said. No threats, just the facts.

He knew. He knew he had me and that I couldn't fight him off, and if I screamed no one would come for me. He had me, but that wouldn't stop me from making it hard for him.

I arched my back and pushed him off me, slamming my legs together, and he slapped me hard across the face. I caught his gaze, his eyes wild with hatred and desire. Anger filled me and I spat in his face. He laughed but it was dark and menacing. I think that was what he liked; he liked the fight. I stopped resisting, but I was afraid of what he would do if I refused to give him what he wanted. He took the knife away from my neck, slipped it under the front of my bra, and pulled hard toward him. My bra snapped back to my sides and exposed my breasts. His eyes wandered over my body. I wanted to take that knife and cut his eyes out of his face. Then he took the knife to my underwear and sliced it into two pieces, pulling them out from under me and tossing them over his shoulder.

I couldn't help it, the tears started to flow unrelentingly, not tears of sadness or pain, but tears of anger. He entered my body with so much force my eyes closed involuntarily. My hands gripped the blanket at my sides and a sob escaped my lips. As he moved in and out of me his hand groped at my neck and my breasts and pulled at my hair. I could feel that my hair was wet with my tears. As if taking my virginity by force wasn't enough, he took my dignity by grasping my jaw tightly in his hand and licking the tears off my face. I turned my head away sharply to the left trying to hide my face from him. How could he not let me have my tears? I clenched my eyes tighter, trying to escape into darkness.

Suddenly, Captain Miller was there, in my mind. His beautiful, stern face full of concern, his quiet, full lips whispering, "Don't go," his long, muscular arms holding me close. I stayed there with him in my mind, hiding myself from what was happening to my body, going to a place that Colonel Weaver could not control.

Everything was still now, my eyes still shut tightly, my hands clenched on the blanket at my sides, and my legs pressed together. I could smell the smoke from his cigar, I could feel his presence and hear his breathing. I lay there still as death is still, ravaged, naked in every way. I tried to move, flexing my hands open and closed, and everything came flooding back, I was in reality now. Sickness washed over me. I rolled quickly to my right side, retched and vomited. I coughed a couple of times and held my stomach with my arms, when I felt something hit my back.

"Get dressed," he said.

It was my dress, I grabbed it from behind me and put it to my face and sobbed quietly. I watched Colonel Weaver walk away but I knew he'd stay close; I knew he was waiting for me.

I don't know how long I sat there; it seemed like forever. My body was no longer my body, I was unsteady on my feet, I had blood all over my legs and the tears had stained my face with makeup. I pulled the dress over my head, unable to zip it up in the back, and stumbled out of the tall grass. Colonel Weaver was there in his car just a few yards away. Stupidly, I smoothed out my dress and my hair, wiping the black from my cheeks. I folded my arms across my chest and closed the gap between us. I found myself saying a prayer.

"Please God, let it be over. I want to go home."

At this point he could be taking me to kill me, and in this state, I didn't care, I just got in the car. I sat there leaning away from him as far as I could. He reached out and I flinched. With that stupid, slimy smile on his face, he turned up the radio and began singing along. It was a Spanish love song. I used to think it was a beautiful song, now I hated it. He sang that love song all the way to my front door. The closer we got to my home, the more my hands felt cold, and my heart sped up. He stopped outside my house and began to open his door to get out, but I was already fumbling with my keys. I slammed the car door and was at the top of my steps before he could even get out.

My hands were shaking so badly I couldn't get the key in the door. I was so tense, expecting him to come up behind me, so I turned slightly to be prepared for the onslaught, but he just stood perched next to the passenger door with his arms folded, smiling at me like I was some joke, a show for his amusement. When he noticed I had turned to look at him, he laughed a disgusting laugh that jarred me to my core.

"Well, have a good night. Let's do this again soon."

My key finally turned, and I practically collapsed through my front door pushing it closed behind me as fast as I could. I fell in a heap on the floor. The sobbing started without my say-so and wouldn't stop. I thought of nothing, I saw nothing, I just sobbed.

After my tears had dried, I became aware that I could smell him, his fluids all over me. I stripped my dress off and threw it away from me and started crawling on my hands and knees toward my room. Once I got to the door, I used the door jamb to help myself up. I looked around my room, inhaled deeply and squeezed my eyes shut, allowing another tear to escape, and walked to my shower. I stepped in and turned it on, I am sure it came out cold but I couldn't feel anything, I was only aware because my teeth started chattering. I cranked it over to heat and sat on the floor of the shower letting the water run over me. I scrubbed myself clean once, twice, three times, until my skin was red and irritated. I wanted him off me, I wanted every ounce of him gone from me.

I stood wrapped in a towel, the room full of steam, and wiped my hand across the mirror, exposing my face. We had to talk, her and I. We had to get through this.

"No," she said, "I'm not letting it go, not yet." I didn't

argue with her, I just said, "I'm going to bed." I opened my medicine cabinet and took out three sleeping pills, maybe four, and swallowed them dry, slipped on a nightgown and climbed into bed. I pulled the blanket over my head and let sleep take me.

Chapter 5
Doctor Miller

I could smell the faint aroma of coffee. I rolled over and was reminded by the pain in my hips and pelvis what had happened the night before. I pulled the pillow over my head and hugged it tightly over my face. I didn't know what a hangover felt like, but this had to be it: splitting headache, nauseated, body revolting against me, definitely a hangover. A date from hell followed by date-hangover from hell.

I rolled over again and slid out of bed onto the floor. I looked up at the panel on my wall. Red lights all around except one. The front door. I stood shakily and my head pounded, I was sure I had a concussion. How many pills did I take? Four? Five? I hit the unlock button and all the lights shifted to green. I leaned my head on the panel, the green light reflected on my face probably made me look how I felt, but what I craved was some normalcy. My body wasn't ready to move. I stayed there with my head leaning up against the cold lock panel for several minutes. The cold metal felt good on my head and gave me what I needed to wake up a little. I made my way out into the hall. My legs were heavy and unrelenting. I felt awkward just walking.

As I turned the corner, I instantly noticed a dark figure standing staring out the window, I sensed his eyes on my reflection and I felt his concern. I was, in fact, in my black satin nightgown. hair a total mess, and I am sure dark circles were present under my puffy eyes. I walked past him to the cupboard and took out a mug and tried to pour my coffee. My grip was nonexistent, and the full coffeepot fell from my hands and shattered on the floor in front of me, hot coffee splashed everywhere and all over my legs. A laugh bubbled up and made its way out, though, feeling like a robot I simply turned and walked right through the glass, the mug still in my hand. Halfway to the door I dropped the mug and it too shattered into pieces.

I opened the back door to my deck and the chilly sea air blew through my hair; it was nice even though it made me shiver. I plopped down in a sort of hump onto my chaise longue, the sun was up, and the brightness made my face set in a brooding squint. I tried to find comfort in the coming and going of the waves, something steady and consistent. Before I could fully immerse myself into the rhythm, I heard the door open. I closed my eyes in anticipation, for what I didn't know. Captain Miller stood there, blocking the sun from my eyes, he set something at my feet and squatted down in front of me. I could see he was holding something.

"Are you okay?"

I was suddenly confused, angry, and excited all at once. What did he say? *Say?*

"What?" It came out a little more acidic than I had really meant. He never looked away and spoke very clearly.

"Are. You. Okay?" he asked again.

I looked up at him, the sun so bright I squinted and placed my hand over my face to block the sun.

"Are you okay?" I repeated back to him. "Are you okay?" I said again. Tears were building, threatening to spill over, a sob escaped my lips. I had no control over my emotions at this point.

"Drink this." He handed me a glass, ignoring my sobbing. "It's orange juice."

"Orange juice?"

"Are you just going to repeat everything I say? Drink it, it will help."

I took the glass shooting him the best glare I could manage and started sipping.

"Now sit back, Major Giles, you've made a mess here."

He started grabbing at my foot, the second he had drawn my mind to it was the second I felt the pain, the sting of air reaching a nerve. I must have cut myself when I walked through the glass. He wiped, picked, and blotted while I sipped.

"Is it helping?" he asked, nodding his head toward me.

"What?"

He laughed a bit and shook his head.

"The orange juice, is it helping?"

I didn't want to admit it, but his orange juice was

helping. Everything was becoming clearer. I refused to address the fact that he was talking to me, in case it was just a dream. I contemplated if I should try and start a conversation as he wrapped a bandage around my foot. I had so many questions I wanted to ask but the only thing that came out was: "What did you do to it?"

"It's just orange juice. Now," he said, looking up at me, "are you okay?"

I blinked heavily and couldn't help it, the tears came, robbing me of any anonymity from my emotions. All I could manage was to shake my head, *no*. I put my hands over my face; I couldn't bear him to see me fall apart like this. Suddenly, his arms were around me and I could feel him rest his chin on my head. I began to sob, and he pulled me closer. He didn't speak, he just let me cry while he held me. The silence was comforting, there was no need to fill the air with words.

At some point my body must have run out of tears. My sobs had slowed but his arms around me didn't loosen. He lifted his head slightly and smoothed my hair back and returned his chin to rest there. I inhaled deeply and took him in, the salty ocean air mixed with his scent was like coming home. He leaned back and tried to look at my face, which I hid in his chest.

"Did you just smell me?" He laughed.

"No," I replied, in an obviously guilty tone.

Just then my stomach growled loud enough for us both to hear. I am sure I turned red though I am not sure why, it's not like I could help it. He put his finger gently under my chin and guided my head to look up at him, holding his body just right to block the bright sun.

"Let's get something to eat," he said, as though we were just two friends out for the afternoon.

He was so calm and inviting I would have done anything, followed him anywhere. He had a deep voice and he spoke in a way that could be a hypnotist, his words came out like he was singing a lullaby or reading a sonnet for a lover.

Captain Miller assisted me inside and sat me at the counter. I noticed the mess I had made had been cleaned up, the missing coffeepot was the only proof that something had happened. Captain Miller went to the kitchen while I sat looking at him like *what now?* He pretended to push up long sleeves and rubbed his hands together in fake excitement and that made me smile.

"There's that smile," he said, leaning his hands on the counter and peering at me. My heart skipped a beat, his eyes pierced right into me, a crooked smile played just at the corners of his mouth, I wanted to crawl inside of him and stay there forever. I tried to make myself feel what I should be feeling, strangeness for his total change in behavior with a total lack of explanation. But I was so grateful for it that I dismissed any strangeness and took comfort in it.

"What's for lunch?" he said, walking to the fridge. I could hear him moving and searching. He shut the door with his shoulder and turned to me, with his arms full of food. He started slicing a tomato, then flipped the knife up in the air and caught it behind his back, and then winked at me. Who was this man? I had no clue and yet I felt like I had known him forever.

I watched Captain Miller slice tomato and cheese; I watched him smear bread with mayo and build two beautifully made sandwiches. He sliced them both into triangles and put them on two plates. As he took the plates to the table, he gestured with his head for me to follow him. Just then I realized that I was still totally disheveled and wearing a nightgown.

"Um, can I have a few minutes." I gestured down to myself. He smiled, a big smile showing all his teeth and I wanted to faint, good grief, he really was beautiful.

"Of course," was all he said, nodding toward my bedroom. I stood awkwardly and headed off to make myself presentable.

I got to my room, my brain trying to process everything. I felt like a kid at Christmas wanting to open everything all at once and wanting to save the best for last without knowing which one it was. I had to dig deep into the back of my dresser, but I found a pair of jeans and a plain white T-shirt. It was slightly too big, so I rolled up the arms a bit and tucked it in the front. I yanked a brush through my hair and pulled it into a ponytail. I wasn't much for makeup, but a little mascara can change a girl's life, I brushed some on and was ready to go. I took a deep breath and opened the door.

As I walked out of my room, Captain Miller stood and waited for me. I walked to the table and sat facing him, as we normally were, but today we had switched roles. Today I was the patient, and he was the doctor, today he was helping me, and I was utterly grateful. I could not even imagine what today would have looked like if he hadn't been there, or if he hadn't reached out like he had.

After lunch I went and sat on my couch, pulling my legs to my chest. Today had been full of surprises and here I was surprised yet again when he came and sat next to me. He put his hand on my knee and looked at me, his eyes full of kindness and questions. He made me feel so many things at once.

"Do you want to talk about it?" he asked, taking one of my hands in his and turning it over as though inspecting it, running his finger over my palm. When he glanced back up at me, I was already looking at him.

"I never want to think about it again, and I don't think I can speak the words out loud." Searching my brain for anything to take the focus off me, I remembered that he had been sick the last time I saw him. I had left him sick in bed.

"Captain Miller, I am so sorry. How are you feeling?" I tried to put my hand to his forehead. He grabbed my hand and tucked it tightly into his. My heart, oh how it told all my tells, I found myself glad he couldn't hear it and see right through me.

"Nice try, beautiful," he said, giving my hand a squeeze. "You don't have to say anything anyway I know Ja-Colonel Weaver well enough to use my imagination." I flinched at his name and realized that Captain Miller was about to call Colonel Weaver by his first name. My brow furrowed and I was dying to ask, I wanted to know, but my desire to never talk about him again won this battle and I let it go, just hanging there in the air like bad breath.

"Captain Miller—" I started.

"Today, it's William, or Will, if you don't mind," he

said, giving my hand a squeeze again. So, it would seem, my hand and my heart were directly connected.

"Will." It seemed foreign coming out of my mouth. "Why—"

He interrupted. "Let's not worry about the 'why' for now. What else do you want to talk about?"

I looked around the room as though searching for something to talk about.

"What's your favorite color?" I asked with a smirk.

He looked at me so intensely, deep into my eye, and said, "Green." My heart pounded in delight for I knew at that moment he was talking about my eyes. At any other point, with any other person, this type of thing would have sent me running, trying to escape, but today, with him, I felt safe, and the most unexpected emotion, I felt happy.

"Why are you being so kind to me?" I asked. He had nothing to prove to me, nothing to gain. He could have taken advantage of my delicate state, he could have left, he could have run. I probably wouldn't have put up a fight, my mind was poring over reasons, sifting through all the answers I wanted him to say even though some of them scared me.

"Kindness is catching," he said, and sort of pulled me closer to him. He pulled my head close to him and kissed my hair. My heart pounded and my breathing changed. I could tell he sensed it and must have felt the same because his breathing matched mine.

"He raped me," I whispered into his chest.

His breathing changed ever so slightly, and I could tell

he instantly went from eager to angry. He squeezed me tight against him and I could feel his muscles quiver and flex as he rocked me gently as if consoling a baby. We said nothing for a long time, just embraced. My words echoed over and over again in my head. I hadn't said it to myself, let alone out loud. I felt like I was talking about someone else. I had already distanced myself from what had happened, it felt like years ago.

Captain Miller shifted and pulled away from me, he cupped my cheeks in both hands and looked me square in the eyes.

"I will make him pay." His eyes shifted back and forth between my eyes, and I knew he meant what he said, and that somehow, he would try.

Just then I heard my fax machine beep and start printing. Captain Miller and I looked at each other, reading the other's mind. We both stood and went toward my bedroom where the machine sat on my corner desk. First the cover sheet, I could see Colonel Weaver's name printed on the top. My heart ached, I felt lightheaded. Perhaps I hadn't separated myself from him as much as I had thought. Captain Miller read my body language perfectly and took the message from the machine and read it, then flipped the paper over showing it to me.

REPORT was all it said. He was checking in on me, he wanted to know what I was doing after his attack, gauging my reaction. I would give him nothing. Just then Captain Miller left the room. I could hear him rummaging through some things, while I just stood there, looking at the paper as though something else would appear on it.

He returned minutes later holding his daily paperwork in his hands.

"Fill it out," he said, handing me the papers and a pen. "Presley, we don't want him coming to check in on us."

He was right. I took the pen and smiled. I smiled because I loved hearing him say my name. I had to hold back from asking him to say it again. I jotted down some notes about a false session I'd had with Captain Miller. I glanced over it a second time; it was believable. I put the paperwork in the machine and hit send. I looked back at Captain Miller who was standing behind me. The look that passed between us spoke a thousand words and yet only two: 'good luck'.

He took my hand and let me out to the kitchen. It seemed so comfortable when he touched me, I craved it the moment he let go and I knew, today something had changed that would never be the same again, something inside me opened and took him in, he would always be a part of me. I would never feel whole without him, and I think I had known it the first day I had laid eyes on him so many months ago.

Hours had passed too quickly and I feared the day was coming to an end. The sun was headed toward the western horizon; the light danced through the windows turning everything a beautiful warm color. Trying to take our minds off the one thing we both had so many reasons to discuss, and just as many not to, we had mindlessly started to make dinner. The sun hit his skin. I couldn't help it, I reached out to touch him, I ran my fingers along his arm feeling the soft hair and the veins that stood out just under the skin. I could feel him looking at me, but I kept my focus on his arm. If I looked at him, I might lose my nerve. I continued to run my hand up his arm onto his bicep. He stopped cutting the carrots and placed the knife down and turned to me. He ran his hand up my arm not taking his eyes off me, and my eyes met his. He put his hand on my neck and ran it slowly into my hair, starting to pull me close. Without warning his eyes changed and his face looked pained, scared even, and he pulled away.

Confused, I just went back to what I was doing. The silence was back but this time it wasn't a comfortable silence; I heard him clear his throat as though to break that silence. I wouldn't let the night be ruined; I was determined to fix this.

"That smells good," I said, trying to sound as normal as possible.

He looked at me and smiled but it didn't touch his eyes. I couldn't read him, but I could tell that, like me, he was trying to rescue the evening. We were two adults, letting some almost-kiss ruin the rest of the evening.

He placed two steaks on the hot pan.

"It's about to get better," he said, now smiling widely.

The table was set for two; this time he had set it with us sitting next to each other. The lights were dimmed, we sat there eating and making small talk. He told me some funny stories about him and his brother when they were kids and how they had drifted apart. I shared with him how it reminded me a lot of me and my brother. War tends to tear families apart. My brother and I had entered the program together, but he had deserted, and I had never seen him again, only heard rumors of his desertion. We laughed and talked like we were just two old friends catching each other up on life. It was both incredibly sad and beautiful.

We washed dishes together and I knew he was feeling what I was feeling. He kept glancing at the clock like it was a bomb, an alarm putting an end to our day. I reached out and touched his arm, getting his attention.

"We have tomorrow," I said.

He said nothing in return, just scrubbed the plate he was holding. *We have tomorrow*, those words seemed so simple and yet I knew that tomorrow was never guaranteed. Someone else was in control of our tomorrow.

"I've got this, you've trained me well, Miss Giles." Like he had done, the first meal we had together, I disobeyed and stayed until every dish was clean and dried.

"I know what you need," he said, with a crooked smile. Captain Miller took my hand and led me toward my room. He let go and went into my bathroom and turned on the bath taps.

"My mother used to tell me I had a talent for running the perfect bath," he shouted from the bathroom and motioned for me to come in. The water was running, and he was lighting candles. The smell of bath salts filled the room. He got a towel and my robe and laid them out on the counter. I turned to look at him and say thank you just as he was closing the door behind him. It was almost strange to be alone, even though I usually took solace in it. I took off my clothes, examining my naked body in the mirror, dark bruises had formed on my neck, chest, and thighs, and a gnarly looking knot on my temple. Reminders of the hell I was forced to live with. I moved and turned in the mirror looking at every inch.

I slid into the hot, bubbly water and closed my eyes. Today would be what I would focus on. I remembered the words, the first words Captain Miller had spoken to me, and every word that followed. I inhaled and let relaxation take me, I smiled and remembered it all again. He was right, the bath was a great idea and he had done a fabulous job. It was perfect.

I was right there at that moment that if I had stayed in the tub, I'd have to add some hot water. My toes and fingers were almost pruned. Reluctantly, I got out and wrapped a towel around me. I listened to the draining water while I put lotion on my body. I knew Captain Miller was waiting for me, so I dressed quickly, putting on some sweats and a tank top. I pulled on my robe and went to the corridor. It was empty, all the lights were off, and it felt cold. I turned and went down the hall to Captain Miller's room. The door was half-closed and I pushed it open. He was on his bed, under the cover, turned away from me. I thought to touch him, but his breathing was heavy and deep. I walked over to him, gently put my hand on his arm, leaned in and whispered, "Thank you." Then I left, closing the door behind me.

Chapter 6
Damn You

Waking up had always seemed so mundane, the same thing over and over, the same routine day after day. Although I had taken comfort in that in the past, today was different. I hopped out of bed, threw on my robe, and practically danced down the hallway. Captain Miller had beaten me out there, as per usual, and stood at the window.

"Good morning," I said, walking over to my coffeepot.

I had to use my reserve pot that only made one cup at a time. I took two mugs out of the cupboard and placed them on the counter. I figured I would make one cup and split it between the two of us.

"Coffee?" I asked.

He didn't answer.

"Good morning, Captain," I said, as though he hadn't heard me.

"William?" I asked, slightly panicking.

I walked over to him, his face was stoic, he was just looking out into the distance if only to avoid my gaze.

"Answer me!" I said, anger creeping in.

I felt the urge to finish that sentence with, 'That's an order, soldier,' but instead I bit my lip, holding it in. I looked up at him, tears brimming in my eyes, angry tears, sad tears, everything tears.

"Damn you," I said, more quietly than I had anticipated.

Without thinking, I grabbed two handfuls of his shirt, urging him to look at me. I started banging his chest with my fists, still holding his shirt in my hands.

"Why?" was all I could bring myself to say, over and over.

I could see the pain on his face, not pain from my fists but pain because he was hurting me and still he let every blow hit him without moving, without flinching, as if he felt he deserved it.

I knew he wasn't going to give me what I wanted, he wouldn't give in. Yesterday was over, a memory, possibly even a dream. I looked up at him, his eyes hard and his nostrils slightly flared. I let go of his shirt, sort of awkwardly smoothed it out with my hands, and stepped back. I wanted to run, to flee the situation, and hide. Somehow, I managed to contain the anger that I felt building inside me and I walked away. The twenty steps it took me to reach my door could have been a mile. I knew he wasn't looking at me, his eyes were still set in the distance, but I felt the tension in the air, I felt his desire to look at me and his will not to. I felt it grow with every step I took away from him until I cut that tension with the closing of my bedroom door. I stood there with my back to the door, I leaned back and slid down the door to the floor, I wrapped my arms around my legs and buried my head in my arms. "Breathe," I told myself. I was here again, needing reminders to breathe. The thought that was in my mind was, One step forward and two steps back.

My muscles were jumping out of my skin. I felt shaky and lightheaded as if I'd had too much caffeine and no food. I craved the beach; my running shoes had started that beckoning song. Yes, I thought, normal, routine. I stood up and went for my workout clothes. I got dressed and felt a surge within me as I tightened the laces on my shoes and went for the door. I stopped dead in my tracks. I feared that if I saw Captain Miller again, if I saw his face, I'd implode. I turned and headed for the sliding door in my bedroom. The water came right up to the deck, so I'd have to get creative and be quick. I flung my body over the banister and landed with a thud in the wet sand. I'd only have a few seconds before my feet would be soaked. I ducked my head and ran for it, in a crouch as best I could.

I had left Captain Miller there, unprotected and unlocked. What was I thinking, there would be serious repercussions if he ran. I'd be dishonorably discharged; I'd lose my home and my job. I couldn't bring myself to care much, it just drove me forward. My feet moved, my legs followed, and I was in a full run, down the beach toward the lighthouse.

It wasn't long before I sensed someone behind me, I could hear the footfalls keeping in rhythm with mine, then faster. They were going to catch me. I slid slightly to the right so they could pass me. It was rare, but I had seen other runners on this beach before, so I wasn't nervous. The person came up on my left, but they didn't pass, they just hung slightly behind me. I started to run faster, pushing myself almost to top speed, and still they stayed with me. I turned my head slightly to see Captain Miller at my flank, keeping pace with me. I pushed harder, I was running at full speed now, hurtling down the beach. I don't think I was trying to get away from him, or maybe I was, but the rock jetty that led to the lighthouse was right in front of me, our race was turning into a game of chicken. I think I was trying to get him to cry out to me to stop, but it didn't come. I had reached the end, I was about to run headfirst into a huge rock, and I willed myself to slow.

My legs skidded to a stop and the momentum pushed me to the ground and I rolled in the sand. I just lay there out of breath as Captain Miller stepped in front of the sun, blocking the light. He reached a hand down to help me up. Reluctantly, I placed my hand in his, and he pulled me to my feet. I braced my hands on my knees and took some deep breaths. Captain Miller didn't even seem winded. I glanced up at him, still supporting myself on my knees. Seeing his face gave me another burst of energy and away I went, sprinting down the beach toward home.

He was soon there at my side, keeping up with my pace as before. I half-glanced his way. It was there a half-smirk on his face egging me on and speaking volumes, saying, 'I'm still here.' We ran, in silence but together. I was surprised that I accepted it, maybe it was as it should be. I don't pretend to know why, but I knew that if he felt it necessary then it must have been for good, and in all of this I had learned that he would never intentionally hurt me.

Once we got home, I headed toward my room and glanced over my shoulder to see Captain Miller sitting at the table unlacing his shoes. I thought to make the best of it, and to let him know I had accepted it, even if I didn't understand. I stood in my doorway with my hand on the doorknob.

"Hit the shower, soldier, then breakfast!" I smiled at him, and I could tell he tried not to smile back but I could see it playing there, desperate to come out. His stoic brooding disappeared for just a moment and then snapped right back into place. For that moment I was grateful.

Captain Miller and I fell back into our routine, a daily run on the beach was a new part of it. It had been three weeks since my date with Colonel Weaver, three weeks and yet a lifetime. After our run to the jetty and back, our favorite thing was filling out paperwork over breakfast for Colonel Weaver, who seemed to always be the butt of our silent jokes. We read books, and by we, I mean I read and Captain Miller listened. I hated television, ignorance was bliss and nothing good was on. He tried to teach me how to play chess, which, let's face it, would seem to be impossible without speaking, although I was starting to catch on, though I'm not sure if Captain Miller would agree.

Today as we ran, my mind was wandering. I wasn't really in it. My lack of competition in my step surely alerted Captain Miller that I was somewhere else. Once we reached the jetty he stopped to rest. He never stopped to rest.

"Are you okay?" I asked, a bit out of breath.

With those words I was transported back to that day. I remembered him asking me if I was okay and the acid in my voice when I repeated it back to him. He looked up at me with a grin on his face, and I knew our minds had gone to the same place.

He took my hand, and my heart leaped as he hadn't touched me in weeks, three weeks to be exact. He pulled me toward the rocks, and climbed up onto the first level, looking down at me. I simply pointed to a sign that read, "No climbing on the rocks". He smiled again and reached his hand down to me, which I took, and we climbed to the top. There was a dirt pathway lined with tall grass that led to the blue door of the lighthouse. It looked huge, this close, white stucco with a worn wooden roof, where you could see remnants of red paint. With the new radar there was no need for the lighthouse anymore, but it was historical and beautiful, one of my favorite things on the island. We walked up to the door; it had a large metal brace with a rusted metal lock. Captain Miller reached into my hair, snatching out a bobby pin that held my hair back.

"Are you going to try and pick that lock?" I asked. The look on his face mockingly said, "Psht, try?" I laughed under my breath while he looked around in feigned fear of being caught and proceeded to pick the lock.

In no time at all the lock fell to the ground with a clatter that made me look around to see if someone had heard us. The beach was empty, the streets were empty, we were alone with the lighthouse. We ducked in and the door shut behind us echoed in the darkness. I blinked several times, letting my eyes adjust. A huge, spiral, wrought-iron staircase wound upward about seven stories. The metal was slightly corroded at the joints from the salty air, but it still looked sturdy. It smelled of cold, damp concrete, stale air hung like the ghosts of past lighthouse keepers. Captain Miller took my hand again and we walked toward the stairs. I ran my hand along the wall, it was cold and rough to the touch. We walked upward for what seemed like forever. My legs started to feel shaky. At the top I could see light shining through cracks in the hatch, getting brighter with each step.

We finally reached the top and could smell the salty sea air. Captain Miller lifted the hatch, which caught the breeze and slammed back, echoing below us. As my head cleared the last step a gust of wind blew my hair. Captain Miller pulled himself through the opening at the top, reached down and helped me climb up. We could see for miles. The sun was up, clearing the horizon, the reflection bounced off the water as far as we could see. There was an iron railing surrounding a lamp that had once been encased in glass. Captain Miller motioned with his head for me to follow as he climbed out of one of the broken windows onto the small space between the lamp and railing.

The wind whipped around. It smelled salty and sweet;

it was so beautiful. I stared out across the ocean, it seemed like I was flying, as if I looked long enough, the space would envelop me, and I would disappear altogether. I leaned my arms on the railing and inhaled deeply, closing my eyes. I felt Captain Miller shift next to me and I opened my eyes. He was looking at me; I saw sadness in his eyes. I reached out and took his hand and the look of sadness intensified. I pressed my forehead to his and whispered, "Are you okay?" He put his hand on my cheek, slowly moving it back into my hair, pulling my face to his. With his lips slightly parted he pressed them softly but firmly against mine. He quickly pulled away, searching my eyes. I answered by grabbing his face with both my hands and pushing my lips back to his. His arms wrapped around my waist pulling me close, our bodies pressed together. I had longed for this moment for months, dreamed about how it would be. But it was better, so much better.

I sat down with my legs dangling over the side, my body braced on the iron railing. Captain Miller sat behind me with his legs straddling my body. He wrapped his arms around my stomach and set his chin on my shoulder. I leaned my head on his and inhaled. I could feel him kissing me gently on my head and neck. Time flew, we watched kids flying kites, and people having picnics, I was not a fan of swimming in the ocean, but there were some brave surfers. I talked a lot, it seemed, about meaningless dreams and wishes I'd had for my life, things I never thought would really happen. A wedding, children, a life outside the military. I had always thought I'd be married to my job, I truly never thought I would fall in love.

I think it was hunger that eventually pushed us to leave our little spot at the top of the world. The walk back home was more of a meander, we held hands and walked, swaying from side to side. I couldn't pry the smile off my face, I just kept glancing at him and every time, he was already looking at me. Home was only a few yards away, but something inside me was scared to go back, like we would leave today on the beach, I would wake up and it would be over again. Captain Miller walked a bit ahead of me, I watched him walk to the deck stairs. His long, muscular arms, glowing warm in the setting sun, his dark hair, a little longer than normal, blowing softly in the wind, his blue eyes glinting in the light. This man before me was never a stranger, he was always this familiar feeling that had existed inside me. The moment I had touched him I had felt it but now he was mine, I had staked my claim, he was home. I felt the need to defend that, I had to fix it. In a second, I had processed several scenarios. Maybe we could run, would he go with me? Where would we go? How would we get there? I had a lot to think about, I had a lot to plan.

I was quiet during dinner, but my mind was reeling with my thoughts, forming a plan to be executed. Every plan hit roadblocks, every scenario failed; I was growing frustrated. I sat at the table with my hand braced under my chin, I pushed more food around my plate than I actually ate. Captain Miller took my plate but hesitated by me for a moment. He looked different than he had all day. He paused, looking at me, then took the plates to the sink.

I didn't have all of the details and it was never far from

my mind, but tonight I felt his frustration in his inability to strike up a conversation like a normal person. I could see the tension in his jaw from what I assumed were unspoken words begging to come out.

"Oh, sorry," I said, with my head still resting on my hand. "Thank you ..." I trailed off, distracted by a thought. The lightbulb in my head came on. I was slow, but what was happening came to the forefront of my mind. He was nervous that my quiet regard had something to do with today, I was driving the poor man crazy with my silence. I stood and walked over to him. He didn't turn so I ducked under his arm and slid between him and the sink. I reached up with my hand on the back of his neck and pulled his face down to mine. I kissed him, vigorously trying to convey the way I was feeling about him, calming his nerves with my lips. He ran his hands down my sides, gripping my thighs and pulling my legs around him and sitting me on the counter.

He kissed all down my neck and I wrapped my legs tighter around him. He pulled away, his eyes wild, my heart was pounding, and my breathing was uneven. He then pulled me off the counter and carried me back to the table and sat me on the chair. He put up his hands as if to say, "Stay." I laughed but obliged, reluctantly. I pulled my legs up to my chest, balanced on the chair. I smiled like a little child with an ice cream cone and watched him walk back to the sink and continue doing dishes, but this time I could see the smirk that stayed on his face. I cannot speak for Captain Miller, but that night sleep did not come quickly, and when it did my dreams were oh so sweet.

Chapter 7
Anniversaries

Captain Miller had been with me now for almost a year. I wasn't blind to the fact that we had an anniversary in just a few days. Honestly, the date made me nervous. Other people I am sure were aware of the anniversary as well. A year is usually the longest I will have any one patient. Most had moved on by this point. I would be a fool to think that Colonel Weaver would just go away or forget about us. However, I took solace in putting that man as far from my mind as possible. That morning during breakfast I heard the fax machine beep and start spitting out papers, as if the machine knew what I had been worried about. My heart ached. I thought of all the things it could be and feared what it would be. I tried to hide my worry from Captain Miller. I stood slowly from the table with an awkward smile on my face, he looked at me, eyes wide. I had hidden nothing from him, and he sensed what I was feeling right away.

"It's fine, just eat. I'll go get it."

I stepped away from the table and walked toward my room. As I reached the machine it was still spitting out pages; I picked one up and recognized it immediately— it was Captain Miller's session notes. I picked up all the papers that had already come out, some of them had fallen to the floor. It was all his notes, all the way back to our first session.

I had a large stack of papers in my hands, I would guess about 360 of them. I walked out of the room sorting through them. Captain Miller was standing at the sink and turned to look at me when I walked in.

"I think we might have a problem here," I said, while straightening the stack in my hands and handing it to Captain Miller.

"Colonel Weaver just sent me back every session we've had. Why would he do that?"

He glanced through a few and handed them back. His jaw clenched briefly, but I recognized the look and knew he was anxious about what he was seeing.

"He's sending a message, isn't he?" I asked, but already knew the answer. We stood in silence for a few seconds.

"He's coming here," Captain Miller said, matter-of-factly.

"What do we do?" I replied, trying not to react differently to the sound of his voice.

He turned to walk out of the room. I am not sure if it was his demeanor, or the sound of his voice but I did not follow. I sat down in my living room and started to prepare myself for whenever it was that I was going to have to see

Colonel Weaver again. Over the last few months, I had been able to push that night down to a deep place in my mind. Captain Miller helped but that block was down, the wall was gone, and I was going to be forced to see my attacker again, and I knew there was nothing he or I could do about it. This man was constantly making me feel weak and controlled; it never went away it was just hidden.

I had learned a lot about who I was; I had found parts of me that I didn't know existed. I knew I could find a stronger version of myself; I knew I could find a woman who could face her attacker and show him that he had not won, he had not crushed her spirit. I knew I could, and I was determined to do it. Captain Miller and I had risked everything, we had risked my job and his life, but I didn't regret any of it and I would die fighting for it. Something was coming, a new fight was imminent, it was right there, and we would be ready.

I went to my room and dressed in my uniform, smoothed my hair back into a tight bun, and put on my heels. It felt awkward, tight and uncomfortable. What once had been my everyday now seemed strange and unpleasant. I walked out into the foyer expecting to see Captain Miller at his post like he had been so many mornings before, but he wasn't there. I could hear sound like heavy breathing coming from his bedroom, so I walked back. He was there on the floor doing pushups. I really didn't know what to say, just the thought of Colonel Weaver had disrupted everything. It had taken our quiet comfortable lives and tossed them into a dryer. I wasn't sure if he was trying to gain strength or just take out some aggression, but judging by the fact that he paid no attention to me when I walked up, it seemed like I should leave him to it. I walked back to the living room and sat to wait. Wait for Colonel Weaver, wait for Captain Miller, or just wait for this day to be over.

I don't know what bothered me more, waiting for Colonel Weaver to show up, or knowing that he was probably sitting back relishing the fact that we were just sitting around waiting for him, and being driven insane with his passive aggressive message. Two days passed of unrelenting apprehension. Jumping at every sound, and pacing, so much pacing. Captain Miller was more quiet than normal, if that even makes any sense, the anxiety rolled off him. I almost couldn't stand to be around him, his energy commanded the room, and then sucked the life out of it.

We sat silently at the dinner table. Another day of this tightrope act had passed, finally the tension had gotten to me. I slammed my glass down on the table sloshing its contents out in a splat.

"This is insane!" I said, as Captain Miller jumped a bit. "I can't take this anymore, don't speak, I don't care, but don't do this." I gestured back and forth to him and myself. He just stared at me, eyes wide, mouth slightly parted, but I'd swear he was fighting a smile. I wasn't in the mood for antics, so I played up the drama instead.

"Fine, fine. I'm going to bed." And I couldn't help it, the words came out before I could stop myself. "You just ... just ... think about what you've done and what you are going to do to fix it."

94

Well, there it was, it was out, I was my mother. I briskly turned on my heel and made a break for it. If anything, at least I had broken the tension. As I sat in my bed, propped up on my pillows, book in hand, reading the same sentence six times, I could hear Captain Miller doing the dishes. I wanted to go out and help him and I wanted to flick water at him and have him kiss my neck; I wanted my life back. He finished and I hurried to flip off my lamp. I sunk into my bed. His footsteps hesitated at my door; my stomach fluttered in anticipation, but his steps continued. I had no choice, so I willed myself to sleep, a restless, dreamless sleep.

The next morning, I woke up and dressed as usual. I had no idea what the day had in store for me, and honestly, I probably wouldn't have done anything differently if I had. I walked out into the foyer; it was empty. I was slightly relieved that I had the place to myself. When you make a fool of yourself it is always nice to avoid the person with which you were foolish to. I poured myself a cup of coffee and retreated to Captain Miller's window. I could see why he liked it there so much. You could see all the way to the lighthouse, the view was beautiful, you could imagine you were alone in the world if you stood still and just looked. My solitude was interrupted by the very familiar sound of my gate opening.

The metal screeched and the house alarm sounded: "vehicle approaching."

"Yes, thank you," I said to the house in a snarky tone. Today was Thursday, it could just be a supply delivery. But I knew who it was, I could feel him with every inch he got closer. I knew with every fiber of my being. Colonel Weaver was about to walk through my door. I hadn't even finished my coffee. I wasn't ready for this. Where was Captain Miller? I didn't know if he heard the gate, but he had to have heard the alarm. I wanted to yell for him, but I was worried Colonel Weaver would hear.

The door boomed open and I jumped, even though I knew he was coming. He entered the house alone; he must have told the other soldiers to wait outside. This bothered me, my palms started sweating, and my breathing began to be uneven. Colonel Weaver stopped just inside the door and took off his aviator glasses, his eyes met mine, just briefly, sending my anxiety to full alert. But he just walked past me into the house and looked around.

"Where's the miscreant con?" he said.

I was scrambling to find my voice; I was trying to form coherent words.

"Um." Was that all I could find?

"Um?" he repeated, walking toward me.

"*Um?*" he said again, sternly.

He was almost to me when I heard someone clear their throat. Captain Miller was standing in the hall making his way to the kitchen. Colonel Weaver smirked and walked toward him. Captain Miller walked right up to him; they were standing eye to eye. The tension was thick and almost palpable, it took on its own entity in the room. I had seen this many times with Captain Miller, his nostrils flared, and his jaw clenched. Colonel Weaver matching his energy. The only way I could explain the situation unfolding in my kitchen was that it was like a showdown between two bull elk fighting for territory. I didn't know what to do, so I just stood very still. Who would strike first?

It seemed like an eternity before anyone spoke. Without taking his eyes off Captain Miller, Colonel Weaver called for the soldiers stationed outside the door. The men came inside and stood waiting for their orders.

"Get me my knout, Mr. Miller here has earned himself twenty lashings, it has been about a year since I had any fun."

Twenty? I thought. Twenty? What had he done? I mean, I knew what he had done, his whole demeanor was an act of defiance. I was shocked and scared. I started toward Colonel Weaver. I didn't even get a sound out of my mouth before a soldier I had never seen before took me by the arm. He practically dragged me to my room and pushed me forcefully through the door, shutting it behind him. I knew he was stationed right outside, I knew I was stuck, then the sounds started, the sound of the whip meeting skin and the sound of a man set on being silent, trying not to make a sound but not quite being able to obey, and the sound of an angry man thrusting blows.

I put my back up against the door and clenched my fists at my side and counted. Eighteen, nineteen, twenty, but the whipping didn't stop, twenty-seven, twenty-eight, a hot tear ran down my cheek turning cold as it fell. My body shook with the urge to let out a sob that I held in my stomach, thirty-five, thirty-six. Anger was building, but I was grateful to replace my fear of Colonel Weaver with anger toward him. Thirty-nine, forty. I wanted him to pay, I wanted him dead.

I felt the knob turn, it was pressed into my hip and I jumped out of the way. Colonel Weaver was standing there, his top button undone, and his tie loosened. He had beads of sweat on his forehead. I wanted to jump at him and claw his eyes out, I wanted to turn my gun on him. I had never been violent and was surprised at the emotion I was feeling toward him. He walked into my room, and I backed up with every step he took toward me. "Coward," I said to myself, disappointed that I didn't stand my ground.

"It looks like you've got your work cut out for you with that one, Doc," he said in a sarcastic tone that instantly reminded me of Sidney Gains. I knew he meant the mess he had made and not Captain Miller's mental state. "Unfortunately for you, he's not going to stay." He looked at me, clearly gauging my reaction. I glared back with hatred.

"Come on, *doctor*." His tone had gone from snarky to cynical. "You haven't really done anything." He was walking in circles around me; it wasn't lost to me that his circle was slowly closing in. He was trying to intimidate me, and I hated that he knew he could. "I asked you to get him to speak, he hasn't in a year. A *year*!" He got louder, and I flinched a little. I knew he noticed because his slimy smile was there, taunting me.

"Am I wrong, Major Giles?" He was right next to me now, staring down at me with menacing eyes.

"*Am. I. Wrong?*" he yelled in my face.

"*Yes, you're wrong*," I spat back at him.

A smile grew and grew on his face until it reached his

eyes. He pinched the bridge of his nose and looked at me, his eyes growing more intense, changing his expression.

"That's all I needed to know," he said.

He motioned with his hands for the soldiers to move out, and just as quickly as I had been surrounded by his presence, he was gone, and I felt cold. I stood in my room unmoving until I heard the gate close. I rushed to find Captain Miller.

He was in his quarters, sort of kneeling on one knee, his back hunched, he was bracing himself with one hand on the ground in front of him. There wasn't a lot of blood, which I was grateful for, most of the blows just left welts and only a few had broken the skin. He had some oozing wounds on his ribs and red welts covering the entirety of his back. I rushed to his side and touched him gently where I could find that wasn't completely red and tender.

"Come on, let me get you to the bed."

"What happened?" he asked with a shaky voice.

I was a little surprised to hear him speak.

"Let's make a deal," I said. "Let's get to the bed and then we can talk."

He groaned while trying to stand and almost fell. I flung his arm over my shoulder and together we made it to the bed.

"Lie on your stomach," I said.

"I don't need your help," he said angrily, pain dripping in his tone.

"Well, I didn't ask," I bit back, echoing his tone.

"And I assume you won't take no for an answer then?"

"You've learned, soldier, now lie down."

He struggled a bit and was finally able to lie face down with his hands sort of drooping over the side of the bed.

"I'll be back," I said, walking out of the room.

"I don't need medication," he called after me.

When I returned, I had a bowl of hot, clean water, a clean rag, and a syringe with morphine in that I had hidden in my pocket. Assisting after a lashing was against the rules, but I was doing it anyway.

"Wait," he said. "Please, what happened with Weaver?"

I set the wet rag on his back, and he cringed and moaned in pain, I rinsed the rag and started again while telling him every word as it happened between Colonel Weaver and me. When I got to the end, he asked me to repeat myself.

"You said *what?*"

"I said, he was wrong."

"So, he said I hadn't spoken, and you said he was wrong?"

He groaned again at the touch of the rag.

"Yeah, I mean, I guess, what's wrong?" I wasn't following, but I was growing nervous. What had I done? I never really knew the whole story with Colonel Weaver and Captain Miller. I had never really known the part I was meant to play.

"You just signed my death warrant," he said, defeated.

I hesitated, not sure what to say, not because I didn't know what to say but because I didn't know what to say first.

"Just give me that shot and get out," he spat out.

"Get out?" I repeated.

Angry, I took the syringe, stuck it firmly in his ass and gave it a good squeeze. He clenched his cheeks and flinched, then groaned at the pain from flinching. I stood there and watched him fade out. All my previous emotions had turned to anger. I was angry at Colonel Weaver and now I was angry at Captain Miller, and most of all I was angry at myself. I didn't know what I had done, but I could feel I had changed the course of everything, I had changed his life, our lives, and I didn't know what to do about it. Most of all, I was angry that Colonel Weaver got the better of me, that I let him intimidate me.

I spent the rest of that day tending to Captain Miller's wounds, he was so out of it I found myself trying to get loopy conversations out of him, but his mind was strong, he kept me at arm's length and stayed quiet. I was able to rub some ointments on, which took the swelling down a lot. By the next day he would feel tight and sore but should be able to function relatively normally. Most of these medicines were meant for emergencies and injuries, I wasn't supposed to use them to heal a punishment. I was beyond caring what Colonel Weaver would do to me, I assumed he had already done his worst.

After everything that had happened in this past year, I knew something was wrong, something wasn't right. Colonel Weaver wasn't what he said he was, Captain Miller wasn't what I was told he was. I didn't know what was going on and I wasn't close to figuring it out, but I had finally decided that I had to figure it out. Today, Weaver at least gave me a starting point. I just needed to know how to do it and how far I was willing to go to get there.

Chapter 8
The Calm Before the Storm

Twenty-four hours can seem like a lifetime, yet in the grand scheme of things, it comes down to just one day. The saying time flies when you are having fun has its place, but not this day. Tending to a grown, stubborn man in pain doesn't constitute as much fun, and Captain Miller resisted every treatment. It was like he wanted the pain, like he thought he deserved to feel it. I stayed with him through the night, administering ointments and pain medication. Time dragged on, but at some point during the night, or in the early morning, I had fallen asleep in the chair I had brought into Captain Miller's room. I woke up with a kink in my neck and my hand completely numb. The light was dim, so I knew it was still early and the sun had not yet peeked over the horizon. The room smelled of salve and blood. Captain Miller was sitting up on the edge of his bed hunched over, supporting himself with his hands braced on his legs. His face was soft, but prominent dark circles sat under his eyes.

I stretched my legs out in front of the chair and awkwardly flipped my dead hand to wake it up. Feeling all the tight muscles in my legs and back made me realize what he must feel like. Reading my thoughts, Captain Miller spoke softly, leaning onto the wall with his shoulder for support.

"I'm fine."

He held up one hand as if to tell me to stay where I was, still being stubborn. We sat there in an awkward silence for a few minutes, whatever had been done or undone yesterday was still lingering in the room, and neither of us knew quite how to talk about it. Maybe if someone would just start, we could figure out how to finish. I remembered my words to Colonel Weaver; at the time they had just seemed like an act of defiance on my part. I hadn't realized then that I would unravel everything, and I didn't know how or why.

"Look—" I started.

"About—" he started at the same time.

"You go." I gestured as though he had the floor. He exhaled deeply.

"About yesterday ... I'm sorry," he said, his voice breaking. He cleared his throat.

I got to my knees next to him and grabbed his hand in both of mine.

"I should be sorry," I said. "I didn't understand what I was saying, what I was doing to you."

"Exactly, you didn't understand, therefore I had no

right to be angry with you. And honestly, I knew we couldn't go on like this forever, to just stay here in our mansion by the sea living happily ever after. Weaver never would have let anything close to that happen."

"So, what is the truth?" I asked, squeezing his hand.

"No," he said. "For so long now I have lived my life guarded, having to watch what I do and what I say, I won't do that to you, I won't tell you. The less you know, the safer you are, and that is my first priority."

I put my head on our hands, kissed his hand softly then looked in his eyes. They were red and tired-looking. I would be lying if I said I didn't want to know, I did. I fought the urge to press him for answers.

"I trust you," I whispered, and kissed his hand again. His face changed and his brows furrowed over his eyes, I could tell he was fighting against his emotions.

"I trust *you*," I said again.

"I know," he said.

His expression read, *You shouldn't*, and he pinched the bridge of his nose. He tried to stand. I stood quickly offering my hand, which he took. He groaned and tried to straighten his back.

"Are you okay?" I asked.

"What is it with us and that question?"

"It just proves we care, soldier," I said, putting his arm over my shoulder.

He smiled and together we walked down the hall.

"Surprisingly," he said, "I feel okay. Pretty stiff but that will work itself out."

I made breakfast while Captain Miller sat awkwardly

at the table randomly stretching and posing like he was doing breakfast-table yoga. I carried two plates over and set one in front of him. We sat together at the table, across from each other. It felt more like a business meeting, or a battle briefing. The truth was, a storm was coming. We both knew Colonel Weaver was gathering his proverbial troops and we should do the same. I wasn't sure if it was a war that could be won, it seemed to me like it would be one of those things where no one comes out a real winner.

"What are we going to do?" I asked, breaking the silence.

I had interrupted a thought, but instantly he was there with me, the thought had disappeared. I watched it leave his eyes. I hadn't meant it to come out so dejected.

"I am working on that," he said, obviously trying to comfort me.

"Let's go, we can just see how far we get—"

"That's too dangerous, Presley, remember my first priority?" he interrupted.

I thought to argue but knowing it would get me nowhere, and would waste valuable planning time, I just slumped in my chair like a toddler who got the wrong-colored cup.

"We don't have much time," he said. "He's coming back for me, and soon."

A tight-lipped smile shot briefly across his face, it didn't touch his eyes and it didn't convince me of anything but the internal war that was raging inside of him.

I stood from the table and was walking toward my room to get dressed and try to get some perspective when

I heard him clear his throat. I turned and he was looking at me with an expression I hadn't seen before, nervousness maybe?

"Yes?" I said, trying to telepathically pry it from him.

"I just wanted you to know ..." he hesitated.

"Yes?" I probed again.

"I needed you to know," he amended, "that I love you. I am so madly and insanely and whatever other adjective you can find to go with the way that I am completely out of my mind in love with you."

In true girl-form I put my hands over my mouth, butterflies and emotions swirling inside of me. I said nothing, walked right over to him, and swung one leg over his lap, straddling him. I placed both hands on either side of his face and kissed him. His hands wrapped around my waist finding their way up the back of my shirt, grasping my shoulders. I had to remind myself not to rub anywhere near his back, he was still shirtless. I wanted to touch all of him. I wanted to feel my skin against his.

He stood, taking me with him, sitting me on the table. He softly pushed me back, so I was lying on the table, my legs still wrapped around his waist. He pushed my shirt up, exposing my belly. He kissed softly right above my waistband, and again a little higher, and then right next to my navel. My back arched, and then he stopped. I opened my eyes and he was offering me a hand to pull me up. His eyes were wide and full of desire. Why had he stopped? He kissed me softly, parting my lips with his tongue, but stopped again, then pressed his lips to my ear and whispered, "Just, I love you, for now."

I didn't want to waste this moment again, I sat back and looked right in his eyes.

"I love you too," I said, tears stinging behind my eyes. But I left *I love you* for now and went to my room for a little perspective.

I sat on the floor next to my bed, anxiety bubbled and churned in my belly and tingled in my blood. I touched my belly where he had kissed me, and touched my lips, I could still feel him there. I closed my eyes and pictured every kiss we had ever shared, every touch. I said I trusted him; I was trying to. I had never enjoyed putting my faith in others. But aside from my dog, Alfa, and my parents, I had never really loved anything. He was working on his plan; I was working on the backup plan. I had decided that for Captain William Miller I would do anything, anything. I wouldn't lose him, and I knew there was a plot going on here, there were lies I'd have to unravel and truths I wouldn't want to hear. But my decision was made, if the situation presented itself, I would take it.

My thoughts were interrupted with a knock on my door.

"Come in," I shouted.

The door creaked and Captain Miller stood there peeking his head around the door.

He said nothing but was holding a pair of running shoes dangling from his fingers.

"Hell yeah!" I replied.

There is nothing like a good run to set your mind right. The day had gotten away from me once again, and this time it wasn't due to fun but more to dreading things to come, like going to the dentist for a root canal. I jumped up and headed for the closet.

"Meet me on the deck," he said, and ducked out.

The view was beautiful, the light bounced off the ocean and the sky was pale blue, wispy white clouds danced in the distance. We kept a steady pace, the tide threatening to envelop our feet. The steady heartbeat and the sound of our footfalls in unison was calming and euphoric in comparison to the anxiety-induced heartache from earlier in the day.

We approached the jetty and slowed our pace. I had been running with Captain Miller for months and I could now keep up with his pace much better. We stopped as usual for me to catch my breath. I walked up to him, kissed him quickly on the cheek and said, "Race you back?"

I took off before he could answer. I pushed my legs faster than before. I heard Captain Miller gaining on me. He came to my side and matched my pace. I pushed harder and still he just matched my pace. Home was in view, and I really kicked it into gear, sprinting as fast as my legs could go. Just before I got there, Captain Miller easily pressed forward, moving to the win. I slowed quickly, bracing myself on my legs. My breathing was unsteady, but a smile lit up my face.

"Cheater," I said, between breaths.

He laughed loudly, and despite everything that had happened, I was completely and perfectly happy in that moment. I would die to protect it.

We held hands and walked up to the door. He took my shoulder and turned me toward him. He used his finger to turn my head up to him and kissed me softly. I walked in ahead of him and said, over my shoulder, "Hit the shower, soldier." Like I always said after our run.

"I thought you'd never ask," he said, a smile firmly placed on his face. He walked into my room and then into my bathroom. He opened the shower door and turned the hot water on. I followed behind him watching his every move. He came over to me and placed his fingers under the hem of my shirt; instinctively I raised my arms. He pulled my shirt over my head. We just stood there for a moment, he seemed to be taking me in. Then he reached up and pulled my ponytail holder out, my hair fell down my back.

I was eager to see him, to feel him. I echoed his movements and pulled his shirt over his head. Remembering his wounds, he flinched slightly. He took my hands and placed them on his chest; I could feel his heartbeat. He slid his hands down my back and into my waistband, slowly removing my remaining clothing. I thought that when this happened, I would feel scared or nervous, but I didn't, I only felt like I wanted more. He removed his remaining clothes, then stepped toward me, our bodies pressing together. I could feel all of him touching all of me, I wanted nothing more but to pull him even closer.

He reached behind me, opening the shower door and stepped in, pulling me in after him. The water rushed down our bodies. He pressed me up against the wall, the water wetting my hair and face. I closed my eyes. His hands searched my body, taking in all of the newly exposed skin, we were getting acquainted with one another all over again. I pulled him into me, aching to be closer, wrapping one leg around him. He reached down grasping my buttocks and pulled me up. I wrapped both of my legs around him.

He opened the shower door and carried me out into the bedroom, laying me on the bed. He hovered over me, water dripping off his body and face. My chest rose and fell heavily with breath that I could no longer control.

Our eyes caught each other, he smiled softly, holding my gaze.

"Are you okay?" he asked sweetly.

I reached up, grasping behind his neck and pulling him to me. I whispered, "Yes!"

He positioned his body on top of mine slowly entering me, watching every facial expression closely. His desire to make sure I was okay made me want him even more. Finally, I felt close enough, finally we were one. Our bodies moved together seamlessly, it was like we had been doing this forever, like we were both made to fit together, two pieces of a puzzle.

I lay there on his chest, listening to his slow, steady heartbeat, his hand tracing circles on my back. Silence had been such a normal thing with him, and right now I didn't feel the need to fill the space with words. He kissed my head every few minutes and we would glance at each other and smile. Never in my life had I ever wanted a moment to last forever like I had wanted that right then.

I rolled a little, propping my body onto my elbow and looked at Captain Miller. He reached up, tracing circles down my chest and breasts. He sensed that I was trying to find the words and asked: "What can I do for you?"

I smiled and pulled myself on top of him, kissing his neck.

"Let's do it again," I said, softly biting his earlobe.

He laughed, flipped us over so that his body was on top of mine, and replied, "Now that, I can do."

Chapter 9
The Plan

I woke to the sound of my fax machine beeping. I stretched, and my body felt strange, muscles I didn't know I had were sore. My eyes fluttered open as I instantly remembered the night before. I reached my hand out, searching the space around me. I could feel the warmth from his body. I looked over at him, still asleep. He looked so peaceful; I hadn't seen him look peaceful very often. Captain Miller always seemed to have a brooding, serious look on his face. I pulled myself close to him, tracing my hands around his body, making him stir. As I tucked my head into his shoulder, my first thought was, He was real, it wasn't a dream. I moved my hands to his belly and down, he groaned in pleasure and rolled toward me so we were face to face, and he kissed my nose. Just then my fax machine beeped again, signaling that it was done coming through. Captain Miller then became hyperaware. That sound made everything come back to the forefront of his mind and his eyes opened wide with concern.

I was hoping that we would have more time before the world came rushing back, before my perfect night was over. But as it was the euphoria was done, we had to get back to reality. Captain Miller rolled out of bed, pulling on some sweatpants. I sat up on my elbow watching him walk shirtless over to my desk. The sun was coming through the curtains, creating shadows, and the wounds on his back looked so much better, just the ghost of what had been. He bent over the fax machine and picked up the paper it had spat out. In an instant he crumpled the paper in his hand and pressed it to his forehead, thought for a moment then threw the crumpled paper at the wall. I imagine that if I hadn't been there, he would have shouted some obscenities.

"What is it?" I asked, the fear and uneasiness in my voice not hidden at all. "Will?"

I was pulling on some clothes when he finally answered: "They're my transfer papers." He laughed a short, menacing laugh and turned his back to me. Weaver was going to make this legitimate, or at least appear that way.

"So, he's still pretending then?" I asked, already knowing the answer. He laughed again and looked over his shoulder at me. His expression was intense, I could feel the anger rolling off him from across the room.

"Time for Plan A," he said, very matter-of-factly.

"And that is?" I asked, closing the gap between us.

"We bring Weaver to us." He paused, pacing away from me. "And from the looks of it, it has to be tonight."

The look he shot me changed from emotion to emotion instantly, anger then pain. I got it, we wanted the upper hand, the element of surprise, but how would we get him to come to us? I stood there, pondering the plan without knowing the plan. Captain Miller started busying himself in a way that made me want to scream, *look at me*! He was picking up clothes and hastily making the bed, all while making sure not to make eye contact with me.

I hated this, I hated Weaver, and I hated that I hated him. I had lived a life dedicated to helping people, having respect for others and using my gifts to heal. In one night, Colonel Weaver had taken that from me, he had changed my way of viewing myself and the world. To add insult to injury, he gave me Captain Miller, only to turn around and take him away. I have no doubt that both were malicious and very much serving his larger purpose. The purpose I was determined to uncover.

I wanted to keep things as pleasant as possible, but the truth of the matter was that Captain Miller was driving me crazy. He wouldn't clue me in on the plan, he was flitting around the house collecting things and muttering to himself. I felt like a vacant body just staring after him, trying to be normal. I fought the need for information and tried to put my trust in him. I walked over to the bed and grabbed the sheets out of his hands.

"Stop," I said. "You have to tell me what is going on, you are driving me crazy."

The look he gave me at that point was one I never wanted to see again.

"Later," he said. "Later, okay?"

I didn't really think it was a challenge but the look, that look on his face, said *I dare you to challenge me.*

"I'll be in the greenhouse," was all I said in return.

I went to my greenhouse to talk with my plants; they listened and never talked back. It seemed that of late I had been ignoring them. I got out my watering can and my clippers, but my heart wasn't in it. I could hear Captain Miller sifting through things and walking back and forth. I was distracted. I thought maybe I'd try the kitchen; food can always speak to the soul. I opened the fridge but there could have been empty boxes in there for all I knew, I saw nothing, just stared into the open fridge abyss. I went for what I knew.

"Do you want some lunch?" I asked, holding a plate with two sandwiches.

"No," he said, then stopped and turned to look at me, then at the plates, then back to me. "I mean yes, it's probably best."

He took one sandwich, took a big bite, and walked away.

"Thank you," I heard him say as he walked into my office.

I took my sandwich and went outside, glaring after him with all the intensity I could manage. I sat on the chair I had been sitting in the first time he spoke to me. I had noticed that a few drops of blood from that day still stained the chair. It had so many memories attached to it, good and bad. The sun was just overhead, sending a reflection bouncing off the water in every direction. I closed my eyes and remembered the night before, the way he touched me and how happy I had been, and how good it felt to be that close to him. I wished it could have lasted longer. Oddly enough, in that moment, my mother's voice came into my head: "Anything good is worth fighting for." I ate my sandwich and said under my breath, "Thanks, Mom."

I had fallen asleep, the sun was headed to the west, it was late afternoon, and I was still there alone in my chair, but the umbrella had been opened and propped to block the sun. Captain Miller had been there, always looking out for me, and keeping me in the dark. I glared up at the umbrella as though it was something else entirely. I am not sure exactly how long I had been sitting there, an hour, maybe two. I thought about going back inside but then my sights landed on the lighthouse and my body instinctively stood and walked toward it. I wasn't feeling like running, so I took off my shoes and walked in the surf, the water lapping cold at my ankles. The beach wasn't empty today, I walked past several people, couples and families. I envied them and pitied them all at the same time, but I wanted to be them all the same. I let my mind wander, thinking about sand crabs and mermaids, but the very thing I was trying to push from my mind kept finding its way back. I thought that I knew what I had to do, but the truth is I didn't know anything. I thought of many scenarios, too many to count. I hoped that this time alone, waiting for Captain Miller, would give me the time I needed to find my courage. I had already committed myself to do whatever it took, and I would, even if I didn't know what that was.

I climbed to the top of the rocks at the jetty, dropping my shoes at the entrance to the lighthouse, and made my way up the steep, winding stairs. I climbed out the hatch and onto the railing. A gust of wind blew my hair and I inhaled deeply. I was contemplating the saying: "It is better to have loved and lost than never to have loved at all." I laughed to myself at the sentiment. Before Captain Miller my experience of real love was of that for my parents. I hadn't lost him yet, but for a moment I desired going back to when I was ignorant of love. My parents didn't show each other physical affection. I figured it was due to what they had been through, watching the world as they knew it end and be enveloped in war. To bring a child into it must have been terrible. I am sure that they did what they could to give me the best life possible and I was always grateful to have both parents in my life, many didn't. But they didn't do much to show me what love was, aside from never giving up on your family, and that was enough.

I looked out across the ocean, watching the sun move across the sky, watching the shadows shift and change. A sadness washed over me; a sadness wrapped in anger. Sad that my life was changing for the worse, anger for the reason why. I was moving through my life just fine, existing, as it were. Then Captain Miller was thrust into it, neither of us were expecting what came of it, neither of us wanted it or needed it. But now, I needed him, I wanted him, and I didn't know what to do to keep him. I had been wrapped up in my thoughts and didn't hear Captain Miller until he was right behind me. I jumped when he wrapped his arms around me.

He didn't say anything, he just held me. We looked out across the ocean and breathed the salty air and held each other. The sun started to dip behind the horizon, sending streaks of purple and red reaching out across the sky and turning the clouds to a glowing orange.

"I wish I could paint this," I said, breaking the silence. "That way I could keep it forever and remember this moment."

As Captain Miller kissed me firmly on my temple, I could feel it all slipping away.

"Come on," he said, "let's go eat."

I turned to look at him, questions in my eyes. I didn't have to speak; he answered the unspoken questions.

"We will talk over dinner, okay?"

The walk home went too quickly, like when your weekend is packed with things to do and suddenly you realize it's Monday and you have to start all week over again. Here we were at the stairs to the house and I knew it was starting again—today's Monday.

Making dinner felt odd, I wasn't where I should be in my head. I could tell that Captain Miller was trying really hard to be upbeat. He whistled while he was grilling steaks, but my vegetable slicing was half-hearted. His whistling stopped and he slid under my arm and put himself between me and the cutting board. He reached up and put his hand behind my neck and pulled me in for a kiss. This kiss was intense, the kind where you have to remind yourself to breathe. I set the knife down and wrapped my arms around his neck. The kiss shifted and started to feel too much like goodbye. I don't know if it was in my head, or if it was actually goodbye.

We were interrupted by the smell of burning steaks.

"Oh no, the steaks." I laughed.

"It's Cajun tonight, I'm on it!" he said, grabbing his meat fork.

Luckily a little charring on a streak isn't so bad. I arranged the food on our plates and carried them over to the table where Captain Miller was already seated, waiting for me. I set the food down in our spots and sat myself. Before Captain Miller could even get one bite I said: "Start talking, soldier." I smiled, but I think he knew I was serious; he forced a laugh and ate the food that was already on his fork.

"What I am about to ask you to do is—"

I interrupted, "I'll do it."

"You haven't even heard what I was asking."

"I trust you, remember? If you say it is what needs to be done, I'll do it."

"You see, that's one of the reasons I fell in love with you."

My heart fluttered at the words. I laughed a nervous, girlish laugh and took another bite, chewing slowly.

"Stop stalling, William Miller. Tell me."

"Ouch, she used the full name," he joked, then hesitated. I couldn't read his eyes. I set my fork down and reached across the table, taking his hand.

"Will, I trust you," I said.

"I know you do, I just don't trust that I am doing the right thing here." He paused and then kissed my hand. "I have gone over so many scenarios in my head and this is the only one that doesn't end with both of us being killed.

I have to go, and I am sorry Presley, but you have to stay, at least for now. I will come back for you, I promise."

There was a long silence; we were both taking in his words and imagining what was about to happen, all the possibilities.

"Okay," I said. "So, we make it look like you escaped?"

"Yes," he said, drawing out the word. "It has to look believable. I have to … do things."

I could hear the pain in his voice, I could also hear the truth in it. He couldn't just go, to make it look believable he would have to overpower me, restrain me, hurt me. I smiled as best I could and said, "I've had worse."

He looked at me and I could see tears brimming his eyes, realizing they were threatening to overflow he dismissed them as quickly as they had come. The reality of what he had just said was sinking in. First, he was going to have to hit me, knock me out even. I couldn't do it myself because it would look too obvious to a trained eye. Then he was going to have to tie me up or restrain me, set off the alarm, then walk away and leave me there for Colonel Weaver to find. It had to be believable. Believable to Colonel Weaver. I took a deep breath and he looked at me, squeezing my hand. I pulled my hand away giving him a half-smile.

After dinner we did the dishes in silence, but Captain Miller had turned on the radio. A beautiful Spanish song played. I was drying the last dish when he took the towel, laid it on the table and took my hand, pulling me into the center of the kitchen. He took me in his arms, but all wrong for dancing. I smiled and corrected the way he was holding me; we began to sway back and forth. He pulled me close at the waist and we were cheek to cheek, our bodies in line, perfectly moving to the rhythm of the music.

The next song came on, blasting polka music, and we both laughed. It felt so nice to laugh with him. He took my hand and led me back to my room.

"It's time for me to use my talents again," he said, taking me into the bathroom.

"Another bath?" I asked, already knowing the answer.

He smiled and turned on the water, then went to my cupboard and put oils and salt into the water, and the room filled with the aroma.

"It's like magic!" I joked.

"Don't make fun of the magician," he joked back.

"Are you joining me?" I asked. The hope and desire was obvious.

He walked over to me and put his hands on my hips, he ran his hands up my shirt and pulled it over my head. He undid my bra and it fell to the floor.

"Not this time, my love," he said. "I am going to take a raincheck though."

I finished undressing and stepped into the tub. He really was good at this; who knew it was an actual talent?

"I am going to hold you to that, soldier!" I said, giving him a cheesy wink.

Everything was feeling forced now. I knew he was trying to distract me before the show, and I was trying to let him. The tub filled and I shut off the water. Captain Miller kissed my forehead and whispered, "I'll be right back." And he walked out of the room.

I closed my eyes and sunk down, neck deep, letting the water wash away the day. A childhood memory popped into my head. Two kids in the playground had gotten into a fight that was quickly stopped by teachers. The two kids had agreed to meet up after school to finish the fight when no teachers could stop them. My friend had tried to get me to agree to go, I hated confrontation and begged her to just go home. When she started walking toward the circle of children around the corner from the school, I couldn't let her go alone, so I followed.

Once we got closer, we could hear the children shouting. The closer we got you could discern that some were yelling one child's name and some were shouting the other, some were just shouting. My friend asked me who I thought would win. I was feeling sick to my stomach, and I remember I didn't answer. She pushed through the crowd, pulling me behind her until we had front row seats. The two boys were taking turns punching back and forth until suddenly they exploded into an all-out brawl, going from punching and hitting to wrestling around. Both boys were bleeding, and the sight of the blood made me sick.

I remember my stomach churned and I was afraid I'd throw up so instead I ran. Once the kids were out of sight the tears started and didn't stop until I got home. When I got there, I immediately called out for my mom, but she was at work. My dad asked me what had happened and I reluctantly told him all about it. He told me that it was no reason to cry and that I was afraid because I was vulnerable. It was that day that my dad taught me how to properly throw a punch. When my mom got home, I remember my parents arguing about it. My mom didn't want me to use violence and my dad wanted me prepared for anything. The truth is, they were both right.

I heard his footsteps and opened my eyes; Captain Miller was standing in the doorway. The look on his face scared me and I could see he was holding something. I didn't need to say anything or ask. I knew it was time. I stood and reached for my towel wrapping it around my body. I went to drain the tub.

"Leave it," he said in a harsh voice.

I think he had found his character, whom he needed to be to get this job done and he had to stick with it, not that I could blame him. My heart was pounding. I wondered if this was how a boxer might feel before stepping into the ring. This was all rushing through my head when I suddenly felt self-conscious. I grabbed my clothes in a bundle under my arm, closed the bathroom door and got dressed. I wasn't trying to take my time, but I was shaking and uncoordinated. When I finally opened the door Captain Miller was still standing in the same spot, his being unchanged felt menacing to me, and for the first time I was afraid of him but started walking toward him anyway. Once I got close enough, he looked down, avoiding my eyes.

"I'm sorry," he said quietly.

His eyes quickly rose to meet mine; his were fierce and blank, I could no longer see him in them. His hand rose faster than I was expecting and came down right across my face in an open-handed slap. Instant burning shot across my cheek. What did I think that we would have a conversation first, a polite discussion about how it was all going to go down? My head snapped back, I wanted to look my attacker in the face but before I could get my head into position another blow hit me from the other direction, this time it was by a closed fist. Tears stung in my eyes. I couldn't help but feel betrayed, but I reminded myself who the real enemy was here. A wave of nausea came over me, I am not sure if it was due to the pain or the emotions, maybe both. I stumbled back a few steps; I could taste blood and my eye was already starting to swell. I reached to wipe the blood from my mouth, but before I could put my hand to my face, a third blow came swift and strong. I stumbled backward and almost fell, he caught me by the collar of my shirt. I felt him wrap something around my neck. I flinched at his quick movement and reached up to my neck instinctively trying to pry it away from my throat. I knew he wouldn't kill me; I knew this was a planned act, but my body fought back without being told to. I could feel with my hands that the object around my neck was a belt, he was pulling it tighter, my fingernails were scratching the skin where I was trying to get in between the belt, desperately grasping at anything to stop what was happening. He was too strong; my fight was going nowhere. I could feel the heat of his body so close to me, I reached out with my hands grabbing at anything I could, searching for anything. White started closing in. Finally, I felt some flesh between my fingers and I grabbed with all my might, feeling my fingernails scrape skin from his body. My feet were fighting hard against him, getting heavy now, my moves were slowing, and my vision was fading quickly. I grabbed at the belt wrapped around my neck one last time, my lungs were burning, trying desperately to breathe some air. Just before everything went black, I heard him say, "I will come back for you."

I felt myself fading into darkness, slipping from reality. I felt cold, and then I felt nothing.

Chapter 10
You Again

It's interesting hearing your name in such a way that you understand immediately that whatever is going on around you is not normal or okay. That panicky, desperate plea for an answer. Sound was coming in waves, washing over me like the ocean, there for a moment, and then being drowned out by a whooshing, coming and going like the tide.

"Major Giles!" I heard the voice say clearly now.

"Major, can you hear me?" It asked again followed by a snapping, or clapping ...

I felt like I was in a dream that I couldn't quite wake up from. Were my eyes open or closed? I heard them calling out to me, but they seemed so far away. My senses knew they were there, but my body wouldn't do what I was telling it to do, everything was running in slow motion.

"Is she dead?" a different voice asked.

"No, she's breathing, it's shallow, but it's there. Look, her eye is trying to open. She's here with us," a woman said.

"Get the medic over here!" That voice I recognized. That voice I never wanted to hear again, that voice made me wish I was dead.

"Presley, baby, I need you to open your eyes if you can!" he pleaded.

If I didn't know any better, I would have thought he actually cared whether I lived or died. He was holding my hand. My eyes wouldn't comply, I tried harder, and a slit of light rushed through the crack in my eyelid and I blinked instinctively.

"There she is," the female voice said. "It's okay, Major, you are pretty swollen and bruised, but we will get you fixed up."

Due to the screaming pain in my jaw, I thought I had smiled at her, but at this point I was just grateful that they had stopped making me open my eyes. I felt better with them closed. I did not want to see Colonel Weaver's face, hearing his voice was bad enough. A hot tear ran down my cheek, I felt a hand wipe the tear away and pull me into their arms like a small child.

"It's okay, baby, I will take care of you now," Colonel Weaver said, rocking me gently.

It didn't sound endearing as it should have, instead it sounded manipulative and dripping with malice. I feared him now more than any other moment before. I didn't know what had happened from the time that everything went black to right now. I didn't know how long I lay unconscious. Where was Captain Miller? Was he okay? What would happen now? I squeezed my eyes shut and then winced at the pain. He must have done a number on me, I felt like I'd hit a bus with my face. I tried to speak.

A strange sound came out of my mouth, immediately followed by a burning inferno in my throat and a searing pain in my jaw. My hands grasped at my throat.

"Hey sh, sh, sh," he said. "Easy. That son of a bitch about strangled you to death, beautiful, you're lucky to be alive, we all are lucky you're still alive." Colonel Weaver brushed some hair away from my face. I felt the urge to vomit all over him, it would have been perfect timing to get away with it.

Disgust was building inside me. Had it not been for my splitting headache, my burning throat, and the fact that my jaw felt dislocated or broken, I might have given Colonel Weaver a piece of my mind. Just then, I was saved by the medic who finally showed up to check me out. He ushered Colonel Weaver away from me, quite reluctantly, but insisted that he needed some space.

"I am Doctor Forrester, Major," he stated, while shining a flashlight in my eyes. A doctor? What did I do to deserve a home visit from Doctor Forrester? Things were starting to come back now; my body was slowly starting to comply. With help from the good doctor, I was able to sit up a little, not without my head pounding but at least I wasn't horizontal any longer.

"You have a mild concussion, and I am afraid your jaw might be broken," Doctor Forrester said, feeling with his fingers lightly down my jawline. "Let's get you in to do some X-rays, and I'd like to keep you overnight."

I felt relieved that I was headed to the hospital for the night, my house felt like ground zero, but a hospital seemed neutral. One of the EMT's gave me a little ice pack that fitted over my face like a mask, it felt nice to have the cold on my swollen eyes. I couldn't help but think, here I was again, a year later, in my bedroom surrounded by soldiers and police, flashbulbs going off all around me.

I could hear the wheels of the gurney being rolled in on my tile floors. I welcomed the idea of getting out of this house, away from these people, one in particular. Where was Colonel Weaver? I was suddenly panicked by his absence. As though he was reading my thoughts, he strutted through the door with an air of arrogance that couldn't be hidden or ignored. He stood in front of a soldier that had been stationed at the door, he was talking very close to him with his back turned to everyone in the room.

"Doctor?" he asked, motioning with his hand for him to come closer. "What is going on, where are you taking her?" he said in a commanding tone as though he owned me.

I knew I couldn't speak, I agreed with the doctor on one thing, my jaw was definitely broken. I watched as close as I could until Colonel Weaver took the doctor by the arm and ushered him into the hallway. I closed my eyes, inwardly cringing. Why couldn't he just leave well enough alone? He came back into the room and walked quickly to my side ,taking my hand in his. I wanted so badly to pull away from him, but I resisted.

"You are going to the hospital," Colonel Weaver said,

while pushing the hair from my forehead. "But I will get you the best care possible, and then we will make him pay for this, I promise."

Another tear ran down my cheek, he wiped the tear and kissed my forehead. The tear was for Captain Miller, the tear was in mourning for the life that we'd shared, which was now over. They strapped me down to the gurney and started wheeling me out; there were police everywhere, taking photos and fingerprints. All I could wonder is if we had done enough to convince everyone of what we wanted. If just one person didn't buy it, the whole thing could come crumbling down. Colonel Weaver was still holding my hand, walking beside the gurney as they wheeled me out the door.

"Can I go with her in the ambulance? I am all she has," he asked Doctor Forrester. I flinched at his words.

"Are you okay, beautiful? Are you in pain?" Colonel Weaver asked me. Why, yes, Jason, I am in pain, mental pain brought on by your falsity and lies.

"Colonel, you would be of better use to pack her a bag and bring it to the hospital," the doctor said, his tone firm but guarded. I knew then that Colonel Weaver had gotten under his skin, gotten into his brain. I wondered what he had told him.

Colonel Weaver brought my hand to his face and kissed it firmly, looking at me, searching my face. He brushed his other hand softly down my cheek.

"Wow, he sure did a number on you, didn't he?" he said in a condescending tone.

Then suddenly, like lightning, it hit me, I knew what I

had to do. I knew my plan and I hated it, but I once said I would do anything, and anything was presenting itself. The bull was staring me down and I was determined to take him by the horns. I tried my best to portray adoration in my swollen, bruised face and squeezed his hand. It seemed to work because he stopped the EMT's from lifting me into the ambulance and brought his face down to mine.

"I am going to take good care of you, beautiful," he said, and then let go of my hand.

The EMT's lifted me into the ambulance, and as they drove away, I watched Colonel Weaver get smaller and smaller into the distance until he disappeared from view. I closed my eyes and breathed a sigh of relief that I had a moment to be alone and reflect, but a different type of healing had to happen first.

Chapter 11
The Lion's Den

A series of beeps and whirs followed by a call over the intercom brought me back from my thoughts. I sat on my firm hospital bed, my feet dangling, not quite able to reach the floor. The smell of wet metal and rubbing alcohol was distant and so subtle I had grown used to it. I took a deep breath and exhaled through my nose. My hospital stay ended up being ten days because I had to have my jaw wired shut. That morning the doctor would be coming to take the wire off and see how things were healing. I was looking forward to being able to open and close my mouth again and to going home. It is true what they say, hospital food is exceptionally disgusting when you have to drink it from a straw and suck it down awkwardly through your teeth! I was excited because I knew they were planning to send me home; it was the first time in ten days that they'd let me get dressed in my own clothes. As I dressed, I noticed that my clothes fitted me a little more loosely, I guessed it was from the liquid diet. I had no desire to lose weight, I was excited for real food. I wanted a doughnut, or a cinnamon roll, followed by a cheeseburger and fries.

I sat still, thinking about what food I was going to eat first and decided to get even more ready to go. I went to my bag sitting on the table next to my bed and began packing up some loose items. Colonel Weaver had brought me a bag of clothes and my toiletries; I hated the thought of him rummaging through my things. He had a soldier bring it in for me and while I was happy not to have to see his face again, it gave me anxiety. I hadn't seen him since I watched his figure disappear into the distance from the ambulance window. What was he up to? No one puts on a show like he did that day with his talk and loving actions toward me and then does nothing to move forward with it. He was up to something.

I became aware of the ticking of the clock on the wall, my mind-wandering suddenly interrupted, as if the clock had been silent and just started ticking again to remind me that time was moving on, with or without me. I realized that Dr. Forrester was late, very late. Now my nerves kicked in and I began pacing. I hate being late, even more so I hate waiting for late people. I wished I hadn't looked at that clock, his lateness hadn't bothered me until I made myself aware of it.

I made it two, maybe three, times around my room when I heard footsteps approaching. My stomach lurched at the excitement of getting back to some type of regular life. I walked to the door and peered out. Much to my dismay I saw Colonel Weaver walking toward me with a bundle of red roses. I was slightly less annoyed when I saw Dr. Forrester next to him. The two men walked together chatting back and forth. As they approached my room at the end of the hall, I could hear their voices seemed strained, as if they had been trying to keep an argument quiet. My hands had gotten clammy in just the few seconds it took for them to get there. I wiped my hands on my pants just before Dr. Forrester put his hand out for me to shake it.

"Nervous, are we?" he asked, with a forced smile.

My hand wipe did nothing to hide that fact that my nerves were evident. I gave him a close-lipped grin and said through gritted, wired-shut teeth, "Let's do this!"

I made a point of not making eye contact with Colonel Weaver and he made a point of making his presence known. He walked in and sort of peeked around the doctor as if I hadn't seen him there.

"These are for you!" he said, holding the flowers out in front of him toward my chest. I stood there looking at him not sure where to go from there, but reluctantly took the roses.

"You're mad at me, aren't you?" he asked shooting me a sideways smile. "I'm sorry I haven't been here to see you; I was busy trying to catch your attacker." His smile turned menacing.

His eyes darted back and forth between mine and I knew he was gauging my reaction. I shot him an awkward smile pointing to the wires in my mouth and shrugged my shoulders. Being nice to him was going to be harder than I thought.

"Come have a seat." Dr. Forrester spoke up, patting my bed.

I gladly obliged and sat on the bed facing him. He began probing and running his fingers down my jawline.

"Any tenderness?" he asked.

I shook my head no.

"Any sharp or traveling pains?" he asked.

I shook my head again.

"Let's get this wire off and see what we see," he said, turning his back to me.

He took a tool from the table he had set up while Colonel Weaver was offering me flowers. He slid his fingers in between my cheek and my teeth and inserted the tool. It was awkward while he fidgeted around for what he was looking for. I was aware of Colonel Weaver standing there watching. My eyes darted to him, he was watching with a strange look on his face, everything about that man made me uncomfortable. I felt the wire snip and one side of my mouth was free and I could taste blood on my tongue from where the wire had poked me. The doctor moved to the other side. He found what he was looking for a little easier this time and I was free. I started to open my mouth.

"Easy," the doctor reassured me. "This might take some time to feel better."

I slowly opened and closed my mouth a few times. It felt strange, like they had taken off my jaw and attached something foreign.

"Opening and closing it is one thing, it's applying pressure that will make or break you. You need to eat soft foods for a while and nothing like caramel or taffy for some time." He gave a small, forced laugh that I could tell was fake. His whole personality seemed off, maybe Colonel Weaver rubbed him the wrong way too.

"When can I go home?" I asked, and immediately put my hand to my jaw. It didn't hurt, just felt very strange, I would imagine if I had been in a wheelchair for ten days and tried to stand and walk it would feel the same. My voice was still hoarse from being strangled, which of course sent my mind to Captain Miller. Where was he? Was he okay? My eyes darted to Colonel Weaver, I was suddenly afraid he could read my thoughts.

"Are you in pain?" Dr. Forrester asked, sounding somewhat desperate.

I could have been wrong, considering everything felt strange to me, but it seemed as though he wanted me to say yes.

"No," I said reluctantly. It sounded more like a question.

I was trying to read him and follow his meaning, but I was confused.

"Can I go home?" I asked, clearing my scratchy throat.

"Uh ..." he paused. "Home?" He paused again.

I squinted my eyes and looked at him, again trying to read him. What was going on? Just then I got my answer. What is it that people say? "Don't ask questions that you don't want the answer to."

"You are coming home with me," Colonel Weaver

said, still standing in my doorway. I glanced at his face, which was plastered with arrogance.

"I am going to take care of you," he said, walking toward me.

My first reaction was to scream and run, then another saying danced through my head: "Keep your friends close …" I let the other half of that saying go around and around until it made me giddy. I hadn't realized it, but it was exactly where I wanted to be, in the lion's den.

Colonel Weaver took both of my hands in his and looked at me trying to convey something with his eyes. I took in his features, he looked handsome, arrogant and terrifying. My stomach turned over, fighting against every feeling rushing through me, trying to keep up with my emotions. I finally settled on one emotion by remembering Captain Miller's voice in my ear: "I will come back for you." To see him again, to win this battle and end this war was my ultimate goal. I thought of Captain Miller, and I smiled. Colonel Weaver put his finger under my chin to raise my face to his.

"Does that make you happy?" he asked, in a peculiar tone.

"I am glad to not be alone," I said, because at least that wasn't a total lie.

I was indeed grateful to have my enemy right at my fingertips, to keep him within my grasp. With that I knew that I was going to have to sell this, I was going to have to do better. Colonel Weaver, however, was not an easy man to read, he had proven that to be the case more than once. I had to learn to read him and prove myself to him, and I had no idea how to do either.

"Alright, Doc," Weaver said, still holding my chin between his two fingers, "let's get this show on the road, we want out of here."

Doctor Forrester looked back and forth between Colonel Weaver and me, visible beads of sweat forming on his forehead. He was fidgeting with something in the pocket of his jacket. Before I could ask if he was alright, Colonel Weaver moved quickly across the room and took Doctor Forrester by the arm and escorted him into the hallway. I knew it, I knew there was something off. I could smell a rat. I felt grateful that Doctor Forrester did indeed have my best interest at heart and had issues with putting me in Colonel Weaver's care, and mostly that he was trying to go with his gut even though he must have been scared. I had to do something. I took my bag over my shoulder, grabbed my roses, and walked out into the hall.

"Doctor Forrester?" I asked sounding flirtier than I had intended, I cleared my throat. "I would really like to go with Colonel Weaver now, can we fax you the discharge paperwork, I just want to get out of here." I cleared my throat again trying to dispel the strangeness of my voice.

Doctor Forrester looked at me agape then closed his mouth quickly to hide his dismay. He walked toward me and took my hand in both of his, looking at me with concern.

"If you're sure, it's all taken care of," he said, obviously giving me an out, telling me so simply that he was willing to risk life or limb if I wanted him to.

I leaned in and kissed Doctor Forrester on the cheek and squeezed his hand.

"I am sure, thank you for taking such good care of me. I will be in touch," I said quietly, then gave him a genuine smile.

"I am here," he said, pausing, "if you need *anything*." He emphasized the word anything. I knew I had an ally; I knew in him I had a friend.

Colonel Weaver took my bag and flung it over his shoulder and offered me his arm. I put the roses in my other hand and took Colonel Weaver's arm. This is what it must feel like walking the green mile, walking willingly to your own death, at least that's what it felt like to me. I had just taken the arm of Satan and offered myself willingly. Here we go, I thought, then laid my head on Colonel Weaver's shoulder as we walked down the hall. The light at the end of this tunnel was not comforting but menacing and formidable, growing larger with each step.

"Thank you," I whispered, as he held the door for me and we stepped out into the hot sun.

Colonel Weaver's car was parked right outside the door— the cherry red convertible that he had picked me up in that night. I cringed and hesitated.

"Are you in pain?" he asked, reaching into his pocket. "I've got your pain medication."

"I'm okay," I said. "I will take it when we get home."

"I like you calling my home your home," he said, opening my door for me.

"Your chariot, milady," he said, presenting my seat with his hand.

Colonel Weaver could be such an amazing man, if he wasn't a sadistic bastard. I got in the car and tried to hide the repugnance from my face. Colonel Weaver walked over to the other side of the car, and without opening his door, flung himself over, landing perfectly in his seat, as he had the night of our date. He leaned over, kissed my cheek, and started the car. As we drove out of the parking lot, I couldn't help but feel melancholy. I watched again as a safe place disappeared into the distance with nothing but uncertainty before me.

As we turned a long, wide corner on the road I could see a gate, with a winding driveway that headed up the mountain. There were so many trees, but I could see, some distance up the mountain, a terracotta tiled roof peeking through. We stopped at the gate briefly, but it opened without a code. Colonel Weaver turned to me.

"It opens to my face," he said with an arrogant smile.

He hit the gas and we sped up the hill. The driveway rounded back and forth, trees lining the entire drive, the vegetation was thick and beautiful. We rounded one more corner and the trees opened into a glen. There was a large stone fence lining a grassy knoll with neatly crafted hedges. The house stood three stories tall, about a hundred feet away. It looked as if an English colonial house and a Mexican villa had had a baby. Several windows with dark wood shutters dotted the front of the house. Tall white stucco pillars stood out in front holding up a large porch where the driveway rounded under it. A twelve-foot double front door was made of dark rustic wood with black cast-iron hinges, a large knocker in the shape of a snake chasing his tail and a matching door latch. A snake, I thought, how fitting. Colonel Weaver could see the awe on my face as I took it all in. He hopped out of the car and walked over to open my door.

"Mi casa es tu casa," he said. "Welcome home." He gestured to the house and garden.

I wondered if he really meant that, something told me that once we walked through that door there would be guards and rules, lots of both. Colonel Weaver grabbed my bag out of the back seat and took my roses. He put his hand at the small of my back and ushered me up the stairs. My hair was in a loose ponytail and the yellowed bruises still on my face were ugly reminders of one of the worst nights of my life. I didn't know what was behind that door, but I pulled out my ponytail and fussed with my hair. Colonel Weaver saw my nervous fidgeting and stopped just outside.

"Don't worry," he said brushing his hand down my cheek. "I will make sure you never look like this again." And he pushed the latch and opened the door.

I wasn't sure what he had meant by that, but at this point I had bigger fish to fry. The door creaked open, and a cold gust of air met us. I took one step, then another and I was there, inside the lion's den.

The door clanged behind me reminding me too much of a prison door. I blinked my eyes trying to adjust from coming in from the bright sun. We stood in the foyer; glistening white tile floors, there was a mahogany table positioned under a cascading crystal chandelier, a large gold vase with beautiful fresh flowers sat in the center of the table. They made my roses look like mere trinkets. A marble double staircase with cast-iron banisters and blue carpeting arced up to the second floor in both directions. Directly to my left there was a big, beautiful door that matched the front door and had three locks running down one side, two soldiers were stationed beside it. They were not dressed in American uniforms, I thought possibly Belizean, but most of our allies had adopted our uniforms. Three security cameras were trained on the door. I continued to look in awe as though I was taking in the beauty of the house and not the security measures.

Colonel Weaver was greeted by a well-manicured older man with a thin, black mustache and dressed in a neat black suit. He leaned in and whispered into his ear. The man nodded, took my bag and roses in one hand, and then took me by the arm. It felt a little strange, as though didn't have a choice, even though he was perfectly polite. I wondered what he would have done if I had resisted. I glanced over my shoulder just in time to see Colonel Weaver disappear behind the three-lock door.

The man, who I assumed was the butler, ushered me up the stairs to the right. At the top there was a large potted plant and an ornately framed painting of a woman with the front of her dress open, exposing her breasts, a common theme in most of the paintings, but this one was more vulgar than an old painting would be. It made me uncomfortable to see her posed that way. We turned the corner and walked down a long hallway. I counted doors as I went, we stopped at the fifth one. The black-suited man opened the door and set my bag and my roses down on a chair just inside. His silence was unnerving and caused me to do the same. I said nothing, just walked in taking in my surroundings, and he pulled it shut behind me. All my fears had come bubbling back to the surface when I heard the lock engage. So, I was a prisoner.

Chapter 12

Expect the Unexpected

At least my room was beautiful; a king-sized four-poster bed sat in the middle, surrounded by plush white carpeting. Everything was decorated in shades of white and gold. The furniture was all mahogany with gold accents. I felt like I was in a fancy hotel in the city, the presidential suite, no less. I walked around the room, running my hand over furniture and looking at the view from my window.

I wasn't sure where to go from here; my heart wanted me to escape, but my head knew I had to stay. I needed information. I wasn't even sure what I was looking for, I just had a gut feeling that there was something to find. Pieces of a puzzle had been shown to me and I was determined to put it together and expose something, anything, whatever it was. I got my bag from the chair by the door and proceeded to put the few clothes I had from the hospital away. I opened the top drawer of the dresser in the corner of the room. It was deep mahogany, with ornate gold handles on curved drawers very French-looking. When I opened it, I noticed it was full, so I started to close it when I realized everything in there was mine. The contents of my underwear drawer at home was now here.

I opened them one after another to find them each full of my things. I went to the closet and it was full of my uniforms, neatly pressed and in a row. There were a few additions as well. Several dresses and matching shoes that I had never seen before. On the floor of the closet sat a small dresser, just as beautiful as the other in my room; it was about knee-height with several small drawers and two larger. I knelt and opened one and it was full of bracelets; the other, earrings, and another, rings. Surely, they were just costume jewelry. Then I opened one of the larger drawers and pulled out something lacy, it was lingerie. Both were full of lingerie of every color and style. I shut it a little too forcefully and cringed. I had an idea of what Colonel Weaver had planned for my recovery.

I sat on the floor of the closet with my knees pulled up to my chest. I considered crying, screaming, throwing things, but nothing would come to the surface. It was like I was an empty shell, no emotion, nothing. So, I just sat there, cold and unmoving, for several minutes. Water, I thought. A shower can make anyone feel right again. I stood and looked around the room, I prayed that I had my own bathroom. There was a door on the other side of the bed. I walked around and pushed it open into darkness. I fumbled around until I found a light switch and a warm, white light brightened the room. The floors were the same white marble, a clawfoot tub was at the far end and a glass shower on the other side.

It was beautiful, finally something to be happy about. I opened the cupboard under the sink and sure enough all my toiletries were there. Had he moved my whole house in? Did I even have a house anymore? Maybe this was my eviction notice. What about my plants? I pushed my green friends as far from my mind as I could manage and ran a bath. A soft-looking white robe hung on a hook next to the tub. I cautiously undressed and slipped into the robe. On a small wooden table next to the tub there were candles and bath salts with a cute, decorative golden spoon to scoop them from the elegant glass container. They smelled like lavender, my favorite. I felt like I had been spied on. How did he know all these things about me, or was it just something you would do for a female guest?

Still feeling strange about my surroundings and unsure of what to expect, I dropped my robe and quickly got into the tub, covering my body with bubbles. I had to admit that so much of my stress melted away in the hot water. I closed my eyes and tried to think happy thoughts. I remembered Captain Miller's smile, the smile he would always try to hide from me when I said or did something funny and he didn't want me to know that he was inwardly laughing. I remembered the way he would come up behind me and brush his hands across my belly before he pulled me close while I was making dinner. Then, the happy thoughts went south. I remembered the look on his face before he struck me that first time, the way his eyes turned dark, and I lost him in the reflection of my own terrified face.

My body involuntarily jolted at the memory sending water splashing over the side, my heart was racing, and my breathing became uneven. I gripped the side of the tub trying to find my gravity. I had come to a conclusion that I wasn't searching for, but there it was. I was reluctantly but wholly afraid of Captain Miller, his memory was tainted with fear and pain. Tears began running down my face and I let out a sob. I got out of the tub and quicky wrapped myself in the fluffy white robe. I was holding it tightly against my chest, when I heard a knock on the door.

I wiped my face quickly and tied my robe while walking to the bathroom door. I was so wrapped up in my feelings that I hadn't considered who would be knocking. I pulled the door open to see a soldier standing there with a silver tray containing food. He was a handsome brunette, he had a nice olive skin tone and a slightly crooked nose, it looked good on him, and he seemed so familiar.

"Yes?" I asked. I assumed why he was there, having the tray of food and all, but it seemed strange to just take the food.

"Good evening, Major Giles, I have your dinner. I was told you were convalescing and would prefer to eat in your room," he said, looking unamused at his task at hand.

"You were told that, huh?" I said almost to myself but I opened the door wider and he stepped into the room.

"You seem to find yourself in sticky situations often, don't you, Major?" he asked.

"Excuse me?" I asked, confused.

"Never mind," he said, in a patronizing tone.

He wasn't facing me, but I could see the side of his face, he was mocking me. He was setting up the tray of food, on the table, with his back to me, so I stood there with a dirty look on my face hoping he could feel the glare from behind him.

"Do I know you?" I asked, my tone dripping with disdain.

He turned and looked at me. I squinted and raised my eyebrows, enhancing my point.

"Major Jackson," he replied, with a crooked grin plastered to his face.

I put my fingers to my head as though it helped me think, and suddenly it all came back to me, that night with Sidney Gains. It had been a year ago and I had only met him once.

"Hank?" I asked. "Is that right?"

"Ding, ding," he mocked again.

"Wow," I said, feeling a little embarrassed how I had spoken to him both times we had met. "It seems every time we meet, I have a bad attitude."

"Yet a little worse for wear this time," he said, pointing to my eyes. I had forgotten about my black eyes. They were now yellow and fading, my face looked sallow.

"Yeah," I said, fading out, what else could I say?

"Well, Major, here is your dinner. It looks like we will have more time to …" he paused, "get to know each other." His tone was still stationed firmly at condescending.

"What do you mean?" Was he a doctor, a psychologist like me? It was not my fault I was there, why shouldn't he take out his frustrations on Colonel Weaver?

"I am the officer assigned to you," he said, while finishing setting up my food on the table.

I couldn't find the words and I didn't want to ask what he meant again.

"Why do I need an officer assigned to me?"

"They didn't tell you?" he asked, incredulous.

Was he really asking me that?

"Would I have asked if they had told me, Major Jackson?"

I was starting to get annoyed by his snarky responses and that condescending tone.

"Major Giles, they placed you on medical leave for healing and evaluations pending a full investigation into your time with that captain." He paused, rubbing at his face in obvious discomfort at the conversation. "For lack of better words, you're grounded, Major Giles, and I am your babysitter, at least when Colonel Weaver isn't evaluating you."

Evaluating, is that what they were calling it these days? I had died and gone to hell, Captain Miller killed me, and I literally went to hell. I had Colonel Asshole evaluating me and Major Snarky as my babysitter. This was hell. Major Jackson stood there fidgeting in awkward silence. I rubbed the back of my neck and felt like screaming in his face.

"Thank you, Major Jackson." I walked over to the door and motioned for him to leave. "I look forward to getting to know you."

He walked in my direction and turned to say something to me. Not wanting to hear it, I shut the door in his face.

"Nice to see you again," he yelled from the other side.

Unfortunately for me he got the last word with the sound of the lock.

Urgh, this man infuriated me. I reminded myself that it could be worse. At least I knew I wouldn't be spending 24/7 with Colonel Weaver. I sat down at the table. There was a steaming bowl of soup, a roll, and some juice. I took the spoon, dipped it in the soup and took a taste. It was good, much better than hospital food. Well, I thought, at least there's that.

After dinner, I dressed in my pajamas. It was only seven o'clock, but the day had been more eventful than I had had in days, and I was tired, physically and mentally. Across from the door to the bathroom there was a small bookshelf. I walked over to examine the titles. I figured most of them were from my own bookshelf, but there were some new titles as well. One caught my eye, *A Midsummer Night's Dream*. I had read it before, but it seemed suited to my situation, for perhaps I would wake up tomorrow in my bed, realizing this was all a dream. I could do without the romance, but I opened to page one and began to read.

The book made me want to contemplate things in life; I let it fall on my chest and went over the last year. I wasn't expecting Sidney Gains to turn on me, I wasn't expecting to fall in love with Captain Miller, and I wasn't expecting to make an enemy of Colonel Weaver, but at least this last year had taught me to always expect the unexpected. Now to work on my recovery time, I would start with Major Jackson. Tomorrow would be a new day and I would try to make amends. If I was going to be stuck with him, at least I could make the most of it. With that thought, I let my mind quiet, I turned to my side letting my book fall. My mind wasn't blank but very tired. As I fell into a deep sleep, I now had to give in to my mind, wherever it wanted to take me.

Chapter 13
Can I Trust You?

Iwoke to a knocking on my door. I rolled over and wondered if the knock was real. I couldn't remember where I was. Then the knock came again, a bit louder, and a familiar voice on the other side said, "I'm coming in, Major Giles. I hope you're decent." The sound of a key in the door reminded me of my prisoner status.

Did he wonder why I was being locked in? Do they lock everyone in, or just me?

"Come in," I said, clearing my sleepy throat.

I propped myself up on my elbows and peered at the light coming through the door. He was carrying another tray. He pushed it onto the table next to my dinner tray.

"Looks like you ate all of your dinner, Major, good job," he said, teasing me first thing.

"I didn't ask for a babysitter, okay. Do you think you can dispense with the mockery?" I asked, biting back.

He didn't answer, instead he went over to the window and pushed the thick drapes back, flooding the room with light. I flinched away and covered my head with my pillow.

"Get dressed," he said. "We are going out today. Are you excited?" He clapped his hands together, feigning excitement.

"I guess that's a no on my request then?" I said from under my pillow.

"You know, Major, you shouldn't mumble. People can't understand you."

Unexpectedly, the pillow was flung off my face, and my covers were pulled from my body.

"Okay, Mom," I said. Two could play this game.

He laughed and turned his back to me, and walked out of the room, then poked his head through the partially closed door and said, "Hurry up, Buttercup." I picked up my pillow and threw it at him, but he closed the door before it made contact, and it fell to the floor.

I walked to the closet where the uniforms and dresses were. I was on medical leave so I knew I shouldn't wear my uniform. It was easier when I knew what to wear, what were we doing? I went to the drawer and pulled out a pair of navy-blue athletic pants, and a white fitted tank top. I could play patient; sounded good to me. I went to the bathroom and fumbled through the drawers looking for my little makeup bag. I couldn't find it but under the sink there was a tote. I pulled it out and opened it. It was full of makeup, some of which I didn't even know how to use. I did my best to cover my bruised eyes and slapped on some mascara. I was pulling my hair up into a high ponytail when my stomach growled, reminding me that I had breakfast waiting.

I lifted the silver lid on my tray to find grits with melted butter, cream, and brown sugar. *I think he is trying to fatten me up,* I thought. There was a quick knock on my door and Major Jackson stuck his head in.

"Are you ready?"

"What are we doing?" I asked.

"Major," he said, "don't talk with your mouth full."

I rolled my eyes and swallowed.

"What are we doing? What shoes should I wear?" I asked, pointing to my bare toes.

"Walking, anything is fine. But hurry up before it gets too hot."

The thought of going outside made me happy. I was wishing I was going for a run on my beach, but Colonel Weaver lived on the mountain. Maybe we could be in for some great views. I quickly shoveled three more bites into my mouth, hopped up and grabbed my sneakers from the closet. As I laced them up, I realized I felt happy for the first time in days.

Major Jackson stood by the door, adorned with a black backpack, blue basketball shorts and a tight-fitting white tank top. I couldn't help but notice how muscular he was; my eyes lingered a little too long at his chest and I was afraid he might have noticed.

"Awwe, twinsies!" he said, pulling at his shorts and doing a sort of twirl. "Do you wanna be best friends?" he asked, then batted his eyes at me.

"Does anyone actually like you?" I asked in a monotone, then walked around him into the hall.

He led me down the hall and out through a door, the bright sun filled the hallway and I squinted into the light. I blinked a few times to adjust my eyes, all I could see was vegetation. The house was so big, and I had been inside for twenty-four hours. I was confused, I needed to get my bearings. I could see trees that spanned the whole property, I looked one way and they sloped up, and the other way they sloped down. We were on the east side of the property; the sun was up and peeking through all the trees, landing on the side of the white house. I could feel the heat radiating from the stucco.

"Where to?" I asked, clapping my hands in mock excitement as he had done earlier.

Major Jackson smiled a huge smile filled with straight white teeth. I imagined he had had braces at some point, no one could be born with teeth that perfect.

"Up!" he replied, pointing ahead.

We were on the top floor; I noticed only at that point that we were standing on a back deck with the same wrought-iron banister blocking us in. The stairs wound down five steps to a landing, down another five in a different direction, then five more, creating a spiral. We walked across the lawn toward a clearing in the trees. The grass soon turned to dirt, and I became aware of a trail winding upward through the trees. It wasn't the beach, but my feet lurched forward in anticipation of exercise, fresh air, and beautiful views.

I started forward aware that Major Jackson was keeping pace behind me; I wasn't sure if he was just keeping pace, or keeping track. The feeling of being a prisoner hadn't diminished, and I was sure he was keeping up just to keep tabs. I inwardly rolled my eyes and picked up the pace. It wasn't long before my walk became a hefty hike.

"Are you trying to kill yourself, Major?" he asked, keeping up with me, although I could hear that he was just slightly out of breath.

"Not me, but maybe you," I replied.

The mountain had changed to a steeper incline. I knew that I wouldn't be able to keep up this pace, my hospital stay and lack of nutrition had curbed my stamina.

"Okay, okay, I give up." Major Jackson had stopped, bracing himself on his knees. Thank the good Lord, I thought. At least he was the first to give in.

"Good grief, woman," he said taking deep breaths. "You really are trying to kill me."

"Well, Major ..." I said.

"Woah, woah, easy on the Major, Major. Unless I am in uniform, I am Hank."

I had spent so many years referring to the people around me formally that it seemed strange to be so casual.

"Alright, Hank," I said, as if the words tasted bad in my mouth, "was there a destination?"

He looked up at me, still braced on his knees, and shot me that huge white smile.

"There is definitely a destination."

He slid his backpack off his shoulder, opened it and took two bottled waters out and tossed one to me, then passed me on the path with the water bottle pressed to his lips and motioned with his head for me to follow him. Well, he recovers quickly. I followed, eager to see where he was taking me. We climbed for what seemed like twenty minutes, this time at a slower pace. My mind wandered over the trees and the sounds of the rainforest. Beads of sweat formed and dripped; I used my arm to wipe them away. I could hear something in the distance, the sound was growing louder as we walked. A deep rumble that my mind painted a picture for me, I knew where we were headed, then he suddenly stopped and turned to me.

"What went on with you and that captain anyway?" he asked out of nowhere.

My heart lurched and ached, my eyes dropped and in that same second, I remembered that I had to play a part. I'd slipped and I feared it was too late, did he notice?

"What do you mean?" I asked shooting him a nonchalant look. "You know what happened. If you were assigned to me, I'd assume you've read the report." I put my hands on my hips in an accusatory stance.

"Alright," he said, "fair enough." He let it lie there then turned and headed into the trees. I hesitated for a moment to gather my thoughts and reapply my facade.

"Come on, Presley!" he said, using the same tone I had used when calling him by name for the first time.

Of all the soldiers in the US military I had to get stuck with Major Snarky. What exactly was his purpose with me? I had to remind myself it was probably better than being front and center on Colonel Weaver's radar.

"If you're going to lose those hospital pounds, I'd move my ass!" Major Jackson shouted from the trees.

Better than Colonel Weaver if only by a small margin ...

I rubbed my face with both hands as if to wake from

a bad dream, nope still here, then I couldn't make myself stop, the words were out so I glanced at my backside praying I wouldn't notice any extra weight, exhaled angrily then stomped into the trees after Major Hank.

Once I rounded the corner, I stopped to take in one of the most beautiful sights I had ever seen. There was a clearing where a hundred-foot waterfall created long feathery strands of water cascading down to a glittering pool. Hundreds of smaller waterfalls cascaded down over every stone on either side. A rainbow stretched all the way across the clearing. I was standing twenty feet away and could feel the mist from the falling water, and the smell of moisture filled my nose. Beautiful plants of all shades of green sprouted from every ledge and rock was covered in a fuzzy moss, with orange, red, and yellow flowers polka-dotting the entire mountainside. I walked down to edge; the water glistened with every movement about fifteen feet below me. The sound of the water crashing was almost overwhelming and yet caused a strange sense of silence; if you were to close your eyes you would feel alone in the universe. I had remembered feeling that way once before and I was suddenly filled with sadness.

"There is no reason to get all teary-eyed, Presley, it's just water." He interrupted my serenity by baiting me. "You know, Presley doesn't suit you. For someone as uptight as you, Major is actually pretty perfect. Relax." He dragged out the last word.

I thought briefly about pushing him in, but was interrupted when he stripped off his shirt, his arms stretching over his head, then pulling it free in a crumpled ball. He bent down and started untying his shoes. I should have done it, why did I hesitate, now he would dive in of his own free will. He stood and shot me a taunting glance daring me to follow, then he arched his back and dove in with perfect form, headfirst into the pool making just a little splash. I peeked over to see when he would surface. Soon his head popped up and he brushed the water from his face with his hands and swam to the side.

He climbed the distance to the top and pulled himself to his feet. Unsure if I could trust him not to fling me over the edge, I took a few steps back. He followed my internal fear and quickly took a few steps toward me as though he was chasing me. I put my hands up warning him to back off.

"Look, Hank, I am not well enough to go leaping off cliffs into water, my jaw is still healing," I warned.

He laughed. Why was he just laughing and why were my eyes drawn to his abs that tightened with each chortle? The water was beaded all over his chest and arms, dripping from his dark hair and shorts. I couldn't find words that made any sense, so I just stood there staring at him, the scowl on my face growing in intensity.

"I was right," he said between laughs, "you're wound tighter than my granny's pocketbook." He braced himself on his knees as he had before, holding up one finger, like his laughing had given him a great ab workout.

"Can we just get the hell out of here, Major Jackson?" I felt like a five year old fighting with my older brother now, with my older brother's friend. My tone was dripping with childish sarcasm.

"Whatever you want, princess," he said, pulling his shirt on, then sitting on the grass to put his shoes and socks back on. "Hey, that's it. You are most definitely a princess."

"Princess?" I questioned, and in true five-year-old form finished with, "Honey, I'm the queen."

He laughed a big booming laugh; were we friends, or did he hate me? I honestly couldn't tell. I didn't really want to leave; I just didn't want to be here with him. I watched as he glanced at his wristwatch then picked up the pace.

"Are we late?" I asked, truly curious.

"Not we, you," he said.

We walked back down the mountainside. I wanted to ask what I was late for but didn't want to hear his voice talking down to me, I also figured he would probably not be honest and make up some stupid story just to annoy me. So, there was nothing but the sound of our feet and an occasional sip from a water bottle to keep us company. The walk home went much faster, and I was glad for that. I assumed it was because it was a downhill trek, and of course the anticipation for what might be coming made the time fly faster.

I could see Colonel Weaver's house standing tall at the bottom of the pathway. I wanted so much to feel that comforting draw to home, but it was still like the hospital or a hotel, not quite home. I wondered how long I would be here. I tried to imagine what the next few days held for me and all I could do was draw a blank, my future was unknown and completely out of my control.

I followed Major Jackson up the stairs and waited

while he fidgeted with a ring full of keys to find the right one. A thought occurred to me, that he seemed to be locking people in and out. He found the right one and opened the door for me to enter. The door closed behind us with a clang as we entered the darkened hallway. The smell of food filled my nose and made my stomach growl. Major Jackson didn't say anything but kept side-glancing at me. I almost asked what he was looking at several times but fought the urge and just kept walking.

Once we came to my door he walked in and went to my closet. Again, I wanted to ask questions but just let it play out. He took a dress from the closet an laid it on the bed, then opened a few different boxes containing shoes, he set a pair on the bed next to the dress. I then noticed my room had been cleaned and the bed made was nothing sacred?

"You have lunch with Colonel Weaver in twenty minutes. Don't be late," he said, using a strange tone that I couldn't read. It sounded a bit judge-y.

"I am guessing I don't have a choice in this matter?" I asked, rubbing my arms in discomfort.

The expression on his face changed instantly and he shot me a smile. I looked at him with confusion; I didn't understand the change in behavior. He said nothing, but his face said a million things, the only problem was that I didn't really know what. He walked toward the door, opened it and slipped through, but then peeked his head around before closing it.

"Go with that dress, you can trust me," and then he shut the door behind him.

The sentence didn't make sense in its entirety, it bounced around my head feeling like two separate sentences. "Go with that dress." And then, "You can trust me." But was that the truth? I wasn't sure who I could trust, at this point I didn't trust anyone, not Hank, not Captain Miller, not even myself.

Chapter 14
Here We Go Again

Days never ended well when it involved a date with Colonel Weaver, I doubted that today would be any different. I hated to admit that Hank was right, but the dress he picked out looked fantastic on me. It was an olive-green sun dress with little off-white flowers. It buttoned up the front and hugged me right along my rib cage. He had paired it with some nude-colored heels. I styled my hair down, with a slight curl. I figured from the dress that it was a semi-casual lunch. I was looking at myself once more in the mirror when there was a knock at my door.

"I'm coming in, if you're not decent then you're late," Hank said, opening the door.

He stopped in his tracks and looked me up and down, appreciating his work.

"You clean up nice," he said, then he had to finish with, "but, you aren't much for makeup then?"

This man would be the death of me. I looked quickly in the mirror. I had done a good job hiding the yellow bruises on my face. I had even used a little eye shadow from my new collection, what did he want from me?

"I really hate you," I said, fluffing at my hair, still looking in the mirror, then I saw that Colonel Weaver had entered the room behind Hank. I quickly turned to face him. Hank was suddenly Major Jackson again and saluted Colonel Weaver as he passed by.

"You are relieved for an hour or so, Major," Colonel Weaver said, dismissing Major Jackson from the room with a wave of his hand.

He walked directly over to me like he was an old friend. He placed his hands on my shoulders and ran them down my arms, taking my hands in his. I tried to smile slightly and hide my discomfort in his touch.

"You look better," he said, brushing his thumb under my eye where a dark bruise used to be. "I am determined to get you healthy and agile again."

The tone in his voice sent a shiver up my spine, what could he possibly want with my agility? I let the thought fall through the cracks of my mind, certain that I didn't really want to know that answer. I Instead searched my brain for a normal question that would start this dreaded afternoon.

"Lunch sounds lovely," I said. Lovely, is that even a word people use anymore? "Um, well, I am starving. Where are we headed?" That was better, and hopefully he didn't notice me fumbling over my words.

Colonel Weaver shot me a sly smile seeming to cover

up some unspoken emotion and gestured with his hand for me to exit through the open door. I walked out into the hallway, he followed, and stood at my side offering me his arm. I took it and we walked down the hall together. It was then that I realized how wide the halls were; we walked side by side comfortably. We turned a corner toward the back of the house and walked down some stairs. They were plain wooden stairs, and the walls were white. Many years ago, they would have been referred to as staff stairs. Once we reached the bottom, we found ourselves in the kitchen, it had gray stone flooring that looked to be many years old, the appliances had been updated but I could see the remnants of an old coal stove that had been there before the new gas stove. It was a huge kitchen, like something you might see in a five-star restaurant. People hustled and bustled around with jobs they had been given; they moved around each other like a choreographed dance. I was in awe of the well-oiled machine before me.

My eyes were lingering on the kitchen staff when Colonel Weaver said my name. By the tone in his voice, I could tell it wasn't the first time.

"I'm sorry, I lost my train of thought," I replied, and followed him out the door that he was holding for me.

We walked out onto a patio set against the mountain. Trees shaded it from the afternoon sun. There was a beautifully set table for two. Colonel Weaver pulled out a chair for me and playfully said, "My lady."

I wondered if he was teasing me for my 'Lunch would be lovely' comment. I feigned a laugh and tucked a stray strand of hair behind my ear.

Colonel Weaver stared at me intently, making me question him. "What?" I asked, glancing back and forth from him to the table.

"There is something about you, Presley, my desire, my need for you means something different."

I honestly didn't know what to say, what kind of a response is merited for that comment? I just looked at him with a questioning expression. I was grateful that he didn't require a reply, he just continued with his monologue.

"I've been through woman after woman, I take what I want and then I move on. I have always been satisfied, and then there was you. I had noticed you many times, but you never paid me the attention I deserved. At first it was annoying, then angering, and then I thought of it as a challenge. I needed you to see me, and if you didn't, I would make you see me. I simply took what was rightfully mine. I knew some day you would come to me willingly, and here you are."

He was setting me up for the most perfect and clichéd con that a single woman can commit. I had to try and convince this man that I wanted to be here, that I wanted him, make him trust me, then take him down. But it seemed too easy. He had set up the scene perfectly. Perhaps it was the chase that drew him in, I could not give in too easily. No, this was time to play hard to get.

"Well," I said, leaning back in my chair. "I needed a safe place to be. It seems everyone is out to get me. Are you that safe place, Colonel?" I leaned forward, placing my arms on the table in front of me. He laughed, a chuckle that just faded into the breeze, then took one of my hands in his.

"If you prove to be an asset in my life, I will be whatever you want me to be," he said, then put my hand to his lips. It wasn't a kiss really; he just rubbed my hand gently with his lips.

Just then a woman, neatly dressed in a black-and-white dress, like a maid in an old movie, came to the table. She was holding two of the silver platters that my food had come on to my room. He glanced at her with an annoyed expression on his face. I thought he was going to yell at her and send her away, so I spoke up.

"Oh good, I am starving, what's for lunch?"

She looked at him for approval and he nodded so she set the trays down, one in front of each of us, and pulled off the lids. On his tray was a nice cut of steak, with fries; mine was fish, not my favorite but I am sure he was being conscious of my jaw issues, easier to chew and all. My side was rice—I would have killed for those fries. I eyed his plate like a ravenous wolf. I hadn't realized how much my diet had made my tastebuds feel neglected.

Just as we were about to eat, Colonel Weaver got a phone call, he talked in between bites and with his mouth full. He paid no attention to me, as if I wasn't even there. Probably for the best because I am pretty sure I drooled while watching him take a bite of steak. Somewhere in my head my brain was telling me to pay attention to his conversation. I didn't think he would say anything too incriminating in front of me, but cryptic conversation can mean more than you would know.

"No, it won't work, I've already tried that, we went as far as we could go with it," he said, then his eyes shot to me just for a second. That drew my attention, I was trained in human interaction and body language granted, so was he but sometimes our human nature kicks in whether we want it to or not. Whatever he was saying, it had something to do with me. My ears perked up while I stared at my plate, moving around the fish and rice, I fiddled with a strand of my hair moving it back and forth through my fingers. I was trying to seem nonchalant about his conversation when he abruptly stood up from the table and walked away.

I could hear him muttering angrily from a distance, but I could not make out what he was saying. He took the phone down from his ear and grasped it tightly in his hand, walking toward me. His eyes narrowed and I could see the anger in his eyes.

"Is everything okay?" Before I could really finish my question, Colonel Weaver gripped under my arm, pulling me to my feet. His breathing was uneven, and his stare was ice-cold. He walked quickly toward the house, dragging me behind him. I stumbled over my feet a few times, trying to keep up with his pace. His silence was unnerving, I thought I would prefer it if he was yelling at me. We headed down the hall opposite from where we had come from earlier; there were two huge double doors at the end of the hall, white with gold scrollwork. I knew instantly it was his room. I wanted so badly to dig my heels into the carpet. He opened the door and we entered into darkness. The curtains were drawn, and I couldn't see anything in front of me.

"Even you." He said, not finishing his sentence but staring intently into my eyes.

Then he thrust me by my arm. I stumbled forward until my knees hit something and I fell onto his bed. Before I could right myself, he was on top of me. I knew what kind of strength he had, I knew what he was capable of, and fear filled me. I tried to scoot away but he grabbed my hips and pulled me under him, pinning my hands above my head in the same movement. I was like a rag doll to him. I tried to right my mind, I wanted to connect with him, to get him to trust me. I had to push the fear away. This time was different from the last, it seemed more desperate and yet he was taking the time to look at me. I looked into his eyes and for one brief moment I saw fear in them. This time I was going to fight, but not in the way you would think. I picked my head up off the bed and pressed my lips to his. I wasn't sure if he would hit me, or if I had just made things a lot worse, but he kissed me back vigorously, it caused my jaw some pain, but it was bearable. Still holding my hands above my head, he started to unbuckle his belt.

Slowly he released my hands, which I wrapped around his neck, I arched my body to fake desire, using his legs he pushed my legs apart and I wrapped them around his waist and pulled him closer to me. My heart was pounding, I was on the verge of panic, but I let it drive me forward. I closed my eyes and pictured Captain Miller's face, my William, my love, and suddenly it became easier. I used my body to roll Colonel Weaver over onto his back and pulled my body on top of him. I straddled him and sat up. He had a strange look on his face, it was incredulous and confused. I grabbed onto either side of his shirt and ripped it open, sending buttons flying.

I had remembered finding one of my mother's romance novels when I was a teenager and in one of the sex scenes the woman had done that. I thought in that moment that I was in danger of having fun messing with Colonel Weaver, but I continued with the scene I had read so many years ago. I placed both hands on his bare chest and scratched down to his belly. He seemed to like it because his eyes rolled into the back of his head, but as quickly as his desire had appeared, the anger returned. His eyes snapped back with that irate glare he had offered me when he hung up the phone.

He flipped me onto my stomach then grabbed my ankles and pulled me to the edge of the bed. He wasn't going to let this happen on my terms, he was the master here and that was the way he liked it. He pulled my dress up and tossed it over my back. I felt him pulling on me so violently and I closed my eyes. I didn't think I could pretend this way; his plan was only to violate me and humiliate me in any way he could. I gripped the sheets with both hands as he pushed on me again and again from behind. Captain Miller was no longer on my mind; it would be an insult to put him there now. I thought only of how I would someday get even, how someday I would watch him burn.

Chapter 15
Thou Shalt Not Judge

After Colonel Weaver was done with me, I lay still on the bed while he dressed. I kept quiet and didn't move, hoping he might forget I was there. He got a phone call and answered. I could hear a voice on the other line, but I could not make out what was being said. I was grateful that the phone call distracted him from me for a moment, but then he leaned down and kissed my lips softly, then my nose, and left. I got up from the bed, found a dark corner and sank to the floor.

I didn't know how long I had. I pulled my knees to my chest and rested my head on them. I had cried so many tears because of this man, but this time I kept my tears to myself. I thought about the day, things that were said and the way I felt. I felt like I had betrayed myself in pretending, I betrayed the love I had for Captain Miller. Had I gone too far? I hadn't even gotten anywhere; I hadn't learned anything new. Just then a hard knock on the door and the turning of the handle shook me from my thinking. My stomach clenched and I quickly tried to gather my wits. The door creaked open, and a sliver of light shot across the room, touching the far wall. Someone walked in.

"Gather your clothes and dress in the bathroom," the voice said in a monotone, like a tour guide with a little snark added in. I knew that tone anywhere. Oh no, not him. Anyone but him.

"Quickly now, I don't have all day for this." He walked over and drew the curtains open, flooding the room with light. He glanced at the bed and looked bewildered.

"I'm over here," I said in a small voice.

Although I wasn't sure where I stood with him in the grand scheme of things, he was the closest thing I had to a friend there. I fought the urge to run to him and cry on his shoulder. He turned to see me sitting in a heap on the floor. He stared at me briefly, his eyes widening as though he hadn't expected what he was seeing, then they narrowed as his jaw clenched.

"Figures," he said. He gestured for me to stand and exit the room.

I stood and tried my best to straighten my appearance, a new hurt took over me because of how Major Jackson treated me, but my only option now was to walk out of the room trying desperately to keep some of my dignity. I knew my way back to my room and my pace was that of someone trying to escape without actually running.

"Easy there, turbo, looks like there's still some juice in you," he said in a sarcastic tone.

I stopped dead in my tracks, turned and stared him down like a bull. I had no words. There was nothing I could say to him that would convey the way I was feeling.

"What ... princess?" he said.

All I could do was ball up my fist and give him the best right hook I could muster. His head went to one side with the force. I felt like a total badass, I had never punched anyone before, but I wasn't prepared for the shooting pain in my hand and wrist. I tried my best to hide my discomfort. His eyes shot to mine, they were full of some emotion, I wasn't sure what, and he rubbed his jaw a bit.

"Not bad," he said, "for a girl." He smiled that infuriating crooked smile. "How's your hand?" he asked, the smile widening.

Tears of anger started burning my eyes and I promptly turned on my heel and walked toward my room. Once I got to the door I scooted inside and tried to slam it behind me, but Hank stopped the door with his hand and followed me in. I walked quickly to my bathroom, this time he let the door slam. I pressed my back against it and slid down to a sitting position, letting my head rest on my knees.

"You know, if he was that bad in bed, I can suggest someone else to show you a good time," he said, from outside.

"Just go away," I said.

"You're going to have to talk louder, princess, I can't hear you."

I stood quickly and flung the door open, anger spilling from every pore.

"*Go away!*" I screamed as best I could, my voice broke and I felt pain shock through my jaw, my breathing was heavy and uneven. The look on Hank's face changed just noticeably.

"Sure, yeah, I will be outside if you need me," he said, turning to walk out, and muttering "princess" under his breath.

I shut the bathroom door as he walked away, and the sobs bubbled back up. I didn't fight it this time and let the tears come. Why was I meant to endure this, hell?

I once again found solace in the shower, so often it seemed my only escape. I let the grime and disgust of the day run down the drain. It was nearly impossible to know how my actions had affected Colonel Weaver, it was impossible to know what he was like with other women. I was talking myself into not giving up. I wasn't sure if I was up for the task, but I was starting to feel myself accepting my self-talk. I wasn't giving up. Not yet. I could hear a distant knocking on the door, Man I am popular, I thought, always people knocking on the door. I stood there dripping wet and naked, not in any hurry to see who was at the door. I wrapped myself in a towel and got out, the knock came again.

"Just a minute, I'm coming!" I shouted. I guess I should have been grateful they were knocking and not just barging in, prisoner status doesn't always come with privacy. I dried myself off and slipped into my robe, tying it as I walked to the door, I held it closed in front as though it was going to just burst open at the slightest breeze. The knock came again as I reached for the handle, testing to see if it was locked, it wasn't. I opened the door expecting Major Jackson but was pleased and shocked to see Doctor Forrester standing there.

"Doctor Forrester!" I yelled like an excited schoolgirl and to my surprise I threw my arms around his neck. "I am so glad to see you." Doctor Forrester was older than me, but probably not enough to be my father, he was just as tall as I was too. He was handsome, brown skin and eyes, black hair, graying at the temples. He spoke with a slight Spanish accent and had a deep, pleasant voice.

"I can see that," he replied, with a chuckle, but wrapped his arms around me and gave me a soft squeeze. He quickly released me and pushed me gently into the room, closing the door behind him. He took my face in his hands looking back and forth between my eyes.

"Are you hurt?" he asked, still holding my face.

"My jaw feels much better, but I screamed at Major Snarky, um Major Jackson."

"No, Colonel Weaver, did he hurt you?" he interrupted.

I stared at him, incredulous, for a moment.

"How did you know?" I asked, letting my eyes drop.

"Listen, Presley," he said, still holding my face but lifting my chin so that I was looking him in the eye, "I know what you are planning to do, there are people out there supporting you." He nodded toward the door. "We can't do much."

"Wait, what is going on?" I stepped back and Dr. Forrester released his grip on my face. I hadn't spoken to anyone about my plan, not even Captain Miller. Dr. Forrester closed the gap between us and took both of my hands in his.

"Listen," he said, softly but firmly. "You have to be careful; we can only do so much to protect you." I wanted to interrupt again and pelt him with questions. "You know Colonel Weaver as good as any of us do, he is dangerous. Get the proof and we will help you." He leaned in and kissed my forehead. "Now, I have to go."

"Wait, how do you know any of this, who can I trust, what do I do next?" I asked in a quiet, hurried voice. He smiled and leaned in. "Only you know that," he said in my ear. Then loudly: "Clean bill of health. Keep doing what you're doing." He winked at me and disappeared behind the door.

What in the hell just happened? I stood there, not sure where to go from there. Who was he talking about? Who in this godforsaken place could I trust? I didn't even know Dr. Forrester was here, and now, all of the sudden, there were these people counting on me to get something, but I didn't know what it was, or how to do it. Today had turned out to be something along the lines of dreadful.

I was still standing there when Major Jackson opened the door and peeked his head in. He gave me a quick once-over with his judging eyes then entered slowly, his eyes darting all over the room.

"Can I help you find something, Major Snarky?"

"Ooh, good one," he replied, continuing his surveillance.

"Did you need something or are you just checking if my room is bigger than yours?"

"What did he say to you, Major, the truth?" he said, turning to face me.

"There is such a thing as doctor-patient confidentiality, Hank."

"Listen, Major Giles." Oh my, he was being serious now. "Why was he here? I was told there would be no visitors. Dr. Forrester was not on the schedule, I need to know why he was here, and how he got in for that matter."

He had closed the distance between us, his brow was furrowed and his nostrils slightly flared.

"You should probably calm down, Major Jackson, he just checked on my jaw and asked how I was healing. I wasn't aware that I was a prisoner." I bit back, not hiding the fact that I was completely annoyed at his onslaught of questions.

He looked me in the eyes for a few seconds. He squinted, challenging my answer, then turned slowly and started toward the door.

"You know, I never pegged you as one of Weaver's harem groupies, but I was wrong about that too." He started to close the door and I grabbed it, which made him turn to face me, eyes wide. I shoved the door open and it hit the wall. I walked toward him and got close, pushing my finger into his chest.

"You don't know me, Hank, you know nothing about me aside from what a piece of paper says, based purely on someone else's opinion of something they too know nothing about. So, you can take your bullshit opinion of whatever you think you know, and rot in hell."

We stood eye to eye for what seemed like an eternity. He didn't back up or move, I felt that we would stay there forever in this stand off if someone didn't cut the tension in that room. Thank goodness it was him; he stepped back and placed his hand on the doorknob but turned his head slightly to face me again.

"It's obvious that you don't know me as well as you think you do, Major Giles. And for what it's worth, you really can trust me."

I said nothing in return, and he shut the door.

I quickly gathered my thoughts and promptly dressed. I wasn't sure what was going on, but I knew there was only one way to find out. I learned by experience and that was what I was going to do; throw myself into whatever it was and let the pieces fall where they may. I took hold of the door handle cautiously, as if I was testing it for heat, the truth was, I didn't know what was on the other side of that door. I assumed Major Jackson, standing guard of the scary prisoner. I turned the handle slowly, trying not to make any noise and opened the door open just a crack, I could only see to one side without opening it more but there was no one there, so I opened the door a bit further.

I peered out into the hallway, looked left and right, but it was empty. I slid my body out of the door, still trying to not make any noise. I felt like a spy from an old movie walking on my toes and darting left and right trying to dodge any unseen enemy. I didn't even know where I was going, I just wanted anything to play out, anything but the day-to-day regimen that Colonel Weaver had on my docket. I reached the end of the hall and peered around the corner to the left. I could see the banister that sat above the foyer, and I remembered the three-lock door. I remembered seeing Colonel Weaver disappear behind it and I knew that I needed to get in there. I took a deep breath and prepared myself to make a run for it. I bolted around the corner and ran solidly into another body.

"Oof," I grunted, and stumbled backward.

A very irate-looking Major Jackson held my arm tightly. "I ... a ..." I said, not finding any words.

"At least lie quickly, Presley," Major Jackson said, while dragging me by my arm back in the direction of my room.

I tried to resist by pulling my arm away, but in a quick move, he had me pinned up against the wall. I could feel the warmth of his breath on my cheek.

"I don't know who you think you are, or what you are doing here, but you are in way over your head," he said crossly. His whole demeanor had changed, there was no longer a playful tone to his voice, the snark had been replaced by distaste.

"Look, I know you are some kind of glorified babysitter, but trust me, I can handle whatever is thrown at me. Now let me go," I said, shoving him away from me. He moved quickly again, putting himself in my path.

"You are blind if you think I'm here to babysit you," he said, challenging me with his eyes.

"I could say the same for you if you think I have anything but unadulterated malice for Weaver," I said, pushing against him again.

Just then I heard footsteps and in a little dance, Major Jackson twisted our bodies together, pulled me into a nook in the hallway and blocked me with his body. We were pressed into the corner behind a large plant, our noses almost touching. I could feel the rise and fall of his breath in his chest.

"I want to trust you, I want to like you, I want so badly

to be right about you," he said, in a low, breathy whisper. We stayed pressed together, our breathing increasing with the passing of whoever was walking in the hallway. My only thought was to shush him.

"I don't need you to like me, Major Jackson, but it wouldn't hurt to have you on my side," I said, as I pushed his chest away from me. We stepped back into the light of the hallway; we were alone. A thousand words passed between us in a single glance. I knew then that, somehow, we were both on the same side. I knew he knew things, which I needed to know and that we were two players in the same game and neither of us had known the other was in play, both just a seeming thorn in each other's side. I knew it had gone all the way back to when he came to collect Sidney Gains from my house a year ago. My mind was twisting and collecting clues. We stared at each other for a moment when I offered him my arm, he took it and escorted me back to my room.

Chapter 16

Let the Games Begin

It is a strange feeling engaging in espionage, playing both sides, and sleuthing. Strange and full of anxiety. I had to start focusing on my gut. I still didn't know who I could trust or how deep everything went. I wondered if Colonel Weaver was involved in something shady, but how shady? I didn't know, he seemed like the type to be running an underground gambling or prostitution ring. But Major Jackson had been placed here by the US Army, I couldn't imagine them caring too much about any of that, it seemed they would just bust in and close it down. I wasn't sure where Dr. Forrester came in, but it seemed that Hank and Dr. Forrester weren't aware of each other in this twisted game, and I definitely knew the army was not sure where I stood. At this point I figured it best to be a silent pawn, maybe fly under their radar, and Colonel Weaver's radar.

It had been three days since Major Jackson and I collided in the hallway. After he took me back to my room, he left, and I hadn't seen him since. I had been reassigned a different babysitter who didn't speak to me, but not like Captain Miller didn't speak, it was as if he was too good to speak to me. I had been informed that I had my court martial this morning, it seems when two of your patients escape violently they have to look into who what when where and how. I was to dress in my uniform and "be ready in fifteen minutes". I hadn't worn my uniform in over a month, it was surreal, and yet it felt good.

I was looking at myself in the full-length mirror on the back of my bathroom door when I heard the door open. Two soldiers entered followed by Colonel Weaver.

"Are you ready, Major? Today is a big day for you, you could get your life back, or end up somewhere else altogether."

I didn't like the way he said that, as if he knew something that I didn't.

"Well, sir," I said, keeping things very professional, "I didn't do anything wrong, so I have to trust that the truth will prevail."

His eyes narrowed in judgment. He said nothing but gestured for me to exit the room. He walked next to me down the hall, flanked by the other two soldiers. We walked in silence and came to the stairs. It hadn't escaped my memory that I was still playing a part. I stopped before heading down the stairs.

"It has been a few days. I was hoping to see more of you," I said, clearing my throat and eyeing the soldiers. "I wanted to talk more about my evaluation before today."

"I have bigger fish to fry right now, Major," he said, while talking my arm to descend the stairs to the foyer. The same two soldiers I had seen the day I arrived were stationed outside the three-lock door. Colonel Weaver made it a point to move quickly through the foyer and out the door. I hadn't been outside in a few days; I welcomed the scorching heat from the sun as we walked the few feet to the car.

As we drove down the mountain, I couldn't help but remember driving here. Time here had passed slowly, it seemed like I had been here an eternity instead of just a couple of weeks. I couldn't make myself be afraid of what was coming, though I thought I should be. I could be discharged or even go to prison if they found some wrongdoing. I felt confident in Captain Miller, and my heart ached at the thought of him. He was fading into a memory and that is what truly scared me. I had pushed him away to protect myself from what would happen if people found out I was in love with him. I closed my eyes and thought of the last words he spoke to me, then silently said to myself, "Any time now, William."

As we pulled up to the courthouse, my stomach reacted to what was about to happen. I put my hand over my belly and tried to calm my nerves. The car stopped and my door was opened. I was grateful for the breeze that blew in. Everyone but the driver got out of the car and escorted me into the building. There was a neatly dressed woman flanked by two soldiers, one man and one woman, standing just inside to greet us.

"You must be Major Giles." The woman smiled and put out her hand to shake mine.

I took her hand and nodded.

"I am Alma Bates," she said, looking back and forth between Colonel Weaver and me.

"Your lawyer," she said, realizing that I didn't recognize her at all.

"Oh," I said, surprised. "I didn't know I had a lawyer, nice to meet you."

"They didn't tell you?" she asked, but Colonel Weaver interrupted.

"It's time, ladies, we can catch up later." He gestured to the clock on the wall.

I was feeling many emotions, but anger was right at the front. I hadn't even talked with this woman; she had never even heard my side of the story and yet she was supposed to defend me to the best of her ability. I was so screwed.

We all stood in front of a desk, the courtroom was full of soldiers, many of whom I recognized from various occasions, and others who I was sure I had never seen before. We got there just in time for the court to announce the judge was entering. Wow, Weaver really timed that just right.

"Please Be Seated." said the judge.

I was pleased to see Judge Andrews in front of me. I had served as a professional witness for several of her proceedings and had a good rapport with her.

"Let's not waste any time, please call the first witness," she said, while sorting through some papers on her desk.

The prosecuting attorney stood and said, "We call Major Hank Jackson to the stand."

My heart jumped. I didn't know why I hadn't seen him

in a few days, my anxiety turned to fear, I really had no clue which way this could go. I realized that I quite literally could have put the nails in my own casket three days ago, and the nausea was back. My pulse started racing as they swore him in.

"Let's keep it to the basics here." the judge said.

"Major Jackson," the lawyer said, "what is your experience with Major Giles?" She gestured to a photo of me on a large screen.

"I met her a year ago when she had an issue with one of her patients," he said.

"Be more specific, Major. What kind of an issue?" she asked.

"One of her mental patients pulled a gun on her, I was one of the soldiers who went to collect him."

This line of questioning went on, asking details of what happened with Sidney. I had to admit this lawyer was really good at making me look bad. But Hank simply answered the questions, and I didn't get the feeling that he was out to get me in any way. I am not superstitious, but I crossed my fingers under the table for good measure.

"Alright, Major Jackson, take us to a year later with the incident with Captain Miller."

My attention was drawn back to the room. My heart rate started to pick up speed. The lawyer put a picture up on the monitor. At first, I didn't recognize who the picture was of, then I realized it was me. The lawyer gestured to the screen and asked Hank if he knew what it was a picture of.

"Yes, that was the state in which I found Major Giles after Captain Miller presumably attacked her."

I cringed and jolted making my chair legs screech on the floor. I put my hand to my temple and rubbed, trying to calm myself down, my breathing was uneven, and it didn't pair well with the nausea.

"Major Giles?" Judge Andrews said. "Are you alright, do we need a recess?"

I thought for just a moment and shook my head.

"No, your honor, thank you, I was just a little taken back, that's all."

"Very good," the judge said. "Carry on."

I listened intently to the remaining questions. I had been unconscious and they collected me and took me to the hospital. I had never seen the damage that Captain Miller had done after I was lights out. I listened to Hank talk about what he saw and what he did. He was the one who had revived me, then left me in the care of a female EMT thinking I would feel more comfortable with a woman. I wasn't even aware of him; I wasn't aware of so many people who were there that day. I felt a twinge of sadness for Major Jackson, he deserved better from me.

Listening to the events from that day, from another person's perspective, seemed strange, it was as though they were talking about someone other than me. My attention was pulled back to the courtroom with the words, "No further questions." She turned to face us making eye contact with Alma, "Your witness."

The prosecutor eyed me with intent. I didn't recognize her, but it seemed as though she was out to get me. I knew in the back of my mind that she was just doing her job and didn't like being in the spotlight. My lawyer walked to the podium and opened a book in which I could see a lot of writing. I had assumed that it was prepared questions for the witnesses. How did she come up with her line of questioning if we had never spoken?

"Major Jackson," she said with authority, "what do you think of Major Giles?"

What? What kind of a question is that? I waited for an objection, but it didn't come. I leaned over and whispered to Colonel Weaver, who was seated next to me, "Can she ask that?" He leaned in close and whispered back, "A court martial is different than civilian court, technically there are no charges filed, they are just presenting evidence and your character is part of that evidence."

I listened for Major Jackson's answer.

"She is very loyal to the army," he stated matter-of-factly.

"Be more specific please, Major."

"Well, she was always good at disclosing everything, she never left any question of her intentions. Very respectful ... " he paused, "... to her ranking officers."

That jab toward me didn't go unnoticed; I had been condescending to him when we had first met.

"In your professional opinion, do you think that Major Giles followed protocol on both days in question?"

Major Jackson leaned toward the microphone, looked at the judge and said, "Yes, I do." His eyes shot to me for a second. I did my best to convey gratitude in that brief moment.

"No further questions, your honor."

That's it? She really has nothing else to ask him? I was starting to get more nervous.

The judge peered over her bifocals at the prosecutor.
"Your next witness then?"
She stood.
"We call Colonel Jason Weaver."
My heart sped up. He stood up, next to me, with his hat tucked under his arm, and walked to the bench to be sworn in. I couldn't imagine the malice he had for me, but I also couldn't find a reason that my being in prison or discharged from the army would benefit him in any way. As I watched Colonel Weaver put his hand on a Bible and sware to tell the truth, I secretly wondered if it was hot to the touch under his hand. The questioning started.

"Colonel Weaver, is it true that you were Major Giles's supervising officer during both instances?"

"Yes ma'am, I have been for eight years now."

"And in your professional opinion, is it like Major Giles to go outside of protocol?"

"No ma'am, I have never personally had experience with that, she has always been a star soldier, a great example of what to do."

I could feel the deceit dripping from every word, not that his words were wrong, but his intent was.

"Colonel Weaver, is it true that you recommended that both Sergeant Sidney Gains and Captain William Miller be sent specifically to Major Giles for treatment?"

"Yes ma'am, she is a spectacular doctor."

The compliments were pouring out of him, as if butter wouldn't melt in his mouth. This type of flattery was disgusting to watch. I knew there would be a catch, he was up to something. It wasn't until three questions later that his intentions became clear.

"Colonel Weaver, do you feel that Major Giles is of sound mind?" I sat a little straighter in my chair.

"Well ma'am, she has been making great progress in my care."

Progress? I was his prisoner; I hadn't received an ounce of care. I had to remind myself to keep my friends close and enemies closer. He wanted me right under his nose, and that is exactly where I wanted to be. My job was becoming more and more clear. I had also been made aware that there were so many others that were involved in this. The prosecutor walked toward the bench, stopped at the desk I was sitting at, and tapped twice right in front of me. It was subtle, but there.

"Colonel Weaver, is it your opinion that if Major Giles spends some more time healing she can make a full recovery and return to services?"

That question, the taps, she was saying: 'I am here for you, I see you, we are on the same side.' My eyes were darting around the room, some soldiers were staring forward looking bored, others staring down at the table, one was playing with a stray piece of fabric on his cuff. The room seemed to slow down. Judge Andrews would glance at me briefly and then dart her eyes away, as did several soldiers in the room, including Major Jackson. I think I was noticing the people on my side, my people. I tried to memorize their faces so that when I saw them again, I would know who to trust.

When they gave the questioning over to my attorney, I paid no attention, it didn't matter. I could only assume I was getting out of there in one piece; unfortunately, that meant I was probably going back into the lion's den. I knew it was going to be the fight of my life. I only had one question and I didn't know who to ask: where is Captain Miller? Someone knew, and I would give anything to just know that he was safe and alive. Colonel Weaver was walking back to the desk, a different expression on his face. Our eyes met and he winked. I smiled as though to play along but my only real thought was that he was going down, one way or another.

Just before we broke for lunch there were three other witnesses: an EMT and two other soldiers who had been there, one from the Sidney Gains incident, and the other from Captain Miller's. I listened to the line of questioning if only for an outside perspective, but Major Jackson and Colonel Weaver were the two most important witnesses because they were there both times. After this was over, I wondered if I would have Hank back as my supervising officer while I was on medical leave.

We returned from lunch and were all standing waiting for the judge to enter.

"You may all be seated," she said, and put on her glasses. "I took some time and went over the testimonies while we were at lunch. I find no reason to continue with any other witnesses and hear the same thing again. It is my opinion that Major Giles has been an exemplary soldier and will continue to serve as an asset to the US military. It is my decision that she will remain on medical leave, under the care of Colonel Weaver as well as her supervising officer, and the protection detail of ..." she paused and looked down at her paperwork, "Major Jackson for the period of one month to gather her wits and get her strength back."

She peered at me over her glasses, pausing for a moment. I had one month to get whatever it was they needed from me, check.

She continued, "At that time, she will be completely reinstated and may resume her work, at her prior residence." She lifted her gavel and slammed it down.

I tried to appear relieved at her ruling. I stood from the desk, turned to Colonel Weaver and put my hand out to shake his. He took my hand, a little too tightly, and the look in his eyes said everything. He had no intention of letting me go after one month; I was going to have to take him down, or one of us would have to die. I was his challenge, his trophy, and he wanted me stuffed and mounted. We walked out to the car that was waiting for us. My lawyer tried to shake my hand, but Colonel Weaver ushered me down the stairs. I saw her staring after me, incredulous.

Colonel Weaver got in the back with me this time and sat close; the other two soldiers stayed behind, so it was just him and me and the driver. Once we were in motion, the glass partition started to go up. Colonel Weaver scooted closer and took my hand.

"I don't want to be the one to tell you this, Presley, but that whole thing was staged. The army is trying to kill you, they had to make it look good, but they want to see you dead for what you did. I will protect you."

I took a deep breath and let it out.

"Honestly, I don't know what to say, everything seemed legitimate to me, and what do you mean 'what I did'? And why would they want me dead?" I knew he was lying; I am not sure what drove me to argue.

"Just trust me," he said angrily. "I have had to pull so many strings to keep you alive, don't ever forget that, Major Giles."

He was very irate. If he had been a cartoon character, I would have seen smoke blowing out of his ears.

"If you are helping me and protecting me, then why am I your prisoner?" I had nothing else to ask, aside from the things I actually wanted answers to.

"I thought you would be smart enough to understand it was for your own protection." He spat the words out, as if it was an insult to my intelligence.

"So, you don't trust me then?" I asked, trying my best to sound innocent to his lies.

"That's enough, I am bored of this conversation." The tone in his voice was enough to make me stop talking, and we sat the rest of the car ride in total silence. As we pulled up to the house, he slid out ahead of me and offered me his hand.

"Don't ever question me again, Presley, I meant what I said."

I smiled a sly smile and took his hand.

"Well, Jason, I guess we let the games begin," I said, and we made our way to the front door. As it closed behind me it felt like certainty, not like a prison this time, but a grave.

Chapter 17
A New Friend

The following day felt different. I sat up in bed with the blankets draped over my legs, the curtains still drawn. I waited for the knock on my door for breakfast. I hadn't slept well, my mind had wandered over everything, not just yesterday or the last year, but my whole life, every decision I had made to get me to that point. I pondered loyalty and love and what they meant to me. I was loyal to my country, and I was loyal to Captain Miller. I loved him and I would do anything to see him again, or I was afraid I might die trying.

The knock on my door came, pulling me out of my thinking. The door cracked open, and a dark figure entered.

"Still in bed, you lazy ass? You think you're some kind of princess or something?" Hank flipped on the light, blinding me, but I could see he was grinning from ear to ear.

I blinked several times; I had never been happier to see him. I balled the pillow next to me and threw it at him. He dodged it with ease.

"Easy on the goods princess, I'm holding precious cargo." He danced around the furniture balancing my silver tray with one hand and set it gracefully on the table next to my bed.

"That smells like real food," I said, flinging my legs over the side of the bed.

Hank lifted the lid and the smell of bacon filled my room.

"Looks like someone performed well yesterday," he said, shooting me a questioning glance.

"I swear, Hank, if that's a sex joke ..." I let my intent trail off and he laughed.

"Easy, princess, I was referring to court," he said, showing off a wide grin, followed promptly by an exaggerated wink.

"Why didn't you tell me that you were going to testify?" I asked, sitting in the chair at the table. That bacon smelled delicious.

"Aww! Somebody missed me!" he said, backing toward the door.

"In all seriousness, Hank, thank you for having my back," I said, taking a huge bite of scrambled eggs. He placed one arm in front and one arm in back and bowed to me like I was a princess.

"I am always serious, princess." He placed his hand on the doorknob and shut the door slowly, then at the last minute stuck his head inside and said, "Just remember, a moment on the lips is a lifetime on the hips."

"I hate you," I said, with a mouth full of food. I wasn't sure what he had thought about me these last couple of weeks, things had been so strained, but I was happy to have the old him back, sarcasm included. I would never admit it to him, but I did miss him.

My stomach felt satisfied and full for the first time in a month. I stretched and went to brush my teeth, and as soon as I had a mouth full of bubbles, Major Jackson appeared in my doorway. I jumped and toothpaste ran down my chin.

"I did knock," he said, pointing to the open door. "Man, where's my phone?" He patted his pockets.

I wiped the spit from my chin with my hand towel.

"Don't you dare," I said, trying to quickly rinse my mouth. Hank was standing there rocking back and forth on his heels. "What's up, Major Happy Pants?"

"Wanna go for a hike?" he asked, snapping his fingers against his palm.

Suddenly I saw why he was so giddy, I too craved that freedom. I was hoping he would take me back to the waterfall, the last time we had been drawn away too quickly.

"I'll wait out here, dress to get wet!"

Out of all the things Colonel Weaver had brought here, I had failed to see my swimming suit. I fumbled through some drawers until I found a long string thingy with a couple of patches of fabric.

"What the hell is this? An eye patch?" I said to myself.

I went back to my clothing drawer's and found a black sports bra and a pair of workout shorts, that would do. I pulled on a tank top and grabbed my tennis shoes.

Hank and I walked next to each other down the hall, this time it felt less like a prisoner situation and more like two friends headed out for the day. Hank had on the same backpack as before.

"Why do we keep doing this?" I asked.

"What do you mean?"

I gestured to our outfits; we had matched again. He laughed, and I nudged him with my shoulder.

"Aww! Someone missed me," I said, using his previous teasing tone.

He fumbled with his keys and opened the back door. As we exited into the heat, he mumbled under his breath, "You have no idea."

It seemed an odd thing for him to say, and I could tell he wasn't really trying to let me hear, so I just let it lie and we started for the trail. We hiked in a comfortable silence for a while, it was nice, it felt free. At some point the comfort became deafening and that feeling of something needing to be said was echoing off the trees like a siren.

"So–" "As–" we both started at once.

"You go," he said.

"As it seems we have things that need to be talked about," I said, trying to be somewhat cryptic.

"So," he said, "I have a place we can talk."

His words made total sense and no sense at all. I mulled them over but didn't push the issue. We came to the fork in the road that I knew led to the waterfall, he went left. Yes! We were going to the waterfall. I could hear the rumble and that smell of water was starting to fill the air. I walked forward with my eyes closed letting the shadows from the trees play on my eyelids with the sun. I listened to the footfall of Hank in front of me, letting my mind empty of everything. When I started to feel the tickle of the water falling lightly on my skin, I opened my eyes.

The sight was just as beautiful as I had remembered. It seemed as though I hadn't been there in months and yet it was only a short time ago. Hank took off his backpack, reached in and tossed me a bottled water. We walked over to the water's edge and peered over the drop. The water was glittering and clear, it looked very inviting. I stripped off my tank top and sat to untie my shoes, I glanced up to see Major Jackson staring at me.

"What?" I said, in an accusatory tone. "I thought we were getting in?"

Hank laughed and pulled his tank top over his head, stretching his arms back and forth, his skin shiny with sweat. I knew he was wanting to jump in as badly as I was. He used his foot to pry off his shoes and then shot me his white, toothy grin, took two steps back and launched himself over the edge. I stood there waiting for him to surface.

"Come on, scaredy pants." I heard from below.

He had surfaced on the other side of the pool, and I had missed it. Alright, I took two steps back and pushed myself off the edge. The fall wasn't far, I went feet first into the pool below. I was instantly caressed with a bubbly burst of cool water over my entire body. I pushed off the bottom and made my way to the surface. When I surfaced Hank was right next to me with a joyful smile on his face. I smiled back.

"Good work," he said. "I knew you could do it." I playfully splashed him in the face with water.

"Don't start something you can't finish, princess" he said, sounding a little out of breath, then gestured with his head for me to follow. He swam toward the falls and dove under; I could vaguely see him behind the crashing water of the falls. I turned my body and swam after him. I dove under, I could feel the force of the water as it tumbled, pushing me down in the water. I wasn't a great swimmer, so it gave me a little anxiety until my head resurfaced on the other side. Hank had pulled himself onto some rocks, water dripping off his extremities. There was a small alcove behind the waterfall. The rock was smooth and gray and clean of any debris. I imagined many people found solace there. Hank offered a hand down to me and pulled me out of the water in a single movement. I sat next to him, ringing out my hair. The air smelled wet and heavy like when it first starts to rain.

"This is beautiful," I said, surprised that my voice was heard over the roar of the waterfall.

"Interesting, isn't it," Hank said, gesturing to the alcove we were in, "how the water traps the sound?"

Hank stood and was pacing a couple of steps in either direction. I looked up at him, he looked as though he was contemplating a serious math problem, his brow furrowed, his eyes confused. It was becoming obvious to me that he still wasn't sure whether he could trust me, and honestly, I couldn't blame him. I stood and faced him.

"You can trust me." I paused and started pacing instead of him. "Honestly. I have to trust you because I need help, I don't know what I am doing here."

I started to get more emotional than expected when I felt his hands on my shoulders. He turned me around and looked into my eyes. My stomach did somersaults in anticipation of what he might say.

He took a deep breath and let it out.

"We suspect Colonel Weaver of treason." My heart jumped at his words; my heart skipped a beat and I had to take a couple of breaths to calm myself. "We have had men trying to infiltrate for months, years even, but somewhere along the line we lose them."

"Lose them?" I asked, confused at his literal meaning.

"Some have, in the long run, joined him, some have mysteriously died of illness, and some have simply just disappeared." His face was serious. "Once we discovered that he had developed some sort of infatuation with you, we figured that a man wasn't needed for the job at all. We just weren't sure if we could pull you in, so we decided to let it play out."

I wanted to feel anger for the danger I had been put in, but I only felt relieved that there was a reason for it, that my pain this last year would not be in vain. I was trying to sort through all the questions bouncing around in my brain. What did I need to know the most?

"How deep does it go? Sergeant Gains? Captain Miller?" I asked, trying to hide the pain in my voice when I said his name.

"We don't know, but we want him to get caught red-handed, with his hand in the proverbial cookie jar, so to speak. We don't want to leave any wiggle room for him to get out of this."

"Why me?" I asked. "How did I get on his radar?"

"We aren't sure of that either. You have known him since you enlisted, correct?" I nodded. "We think it has something to do with Gains or Miller somehow, but we can't seem to find anything solid to follow, it's like the real people have been erased, except for what Weaver wanted us to find."

"Well, I am up for the task. I want to take him down. He took something from me." I trailed off, feeling the emotions from that night and then remembering the words that Captain Miller first spoke to me the following day."

"Are you okay?" Hank asked, echoing my thoughts.

"Strange," I said, shaking my head.

"What is strange?" he asked, putting his hand on my arm. His touch felt nice, I was starting to get cold and his hand was warm.

"You just echoed my thoughts is all. Colonel Weaver has already taken everything from me, he can't hurt me anymore. What do we do next?"

Unexpectedly, Hank closed the gap between us and took me in his arms. I hadn't realized that a tear had spilled over and was rolling down my cheek. I also hadn't realized how much I needed that hug. I wrapped my arms around him and let him comfort me.

"I'm so sorry," he said, "I was too proud to see the truth. I should have protected you."

I stepped back, breaking our embrace.

"It's not your fault, Hank. Let's make him pay for what he has done."

He smiled at me in a way that was putting off the conversation, and said, "Not yet, today we are swimming."

He arched over, bent his knees and dove headfirst through the waterfall into the pool below. I let the conversation lie at the bottom of that cave and I dove in after him.

Chapter 18

No Rest for the Wicked

I woke up to someone shaking me, and a familiar voice encouraging me to get up.

"Presley, we don't have much time, you have to get up."

I swung my legs over the side of the bed and searched for my slippers, my mind was firing but only halfway. Adrenaline was starting to build, driving me forward in the right direction.

"Colonel Weaver and his cronies all left, we don't know why or what happened, but our window might be very small."

I wanted to ask questions but thought it best to just follow orders.

Major Jackson took me by my arm and escorted me into the hallway, the house was dimly lit and quiet. There was no light coming in the windows, it must have been early morning. We moved quickly down the stairs; Hank was using a small flashlight to see. I felt like a burglar lurking in the darkness. I could hear the heartbeat in my ears as we approached the three-lock door. Hank had some sort of kit in his hands. He placed the flashlight in his mouth and started to pick the top lock. I reached up and took the flashlight from his mouth, but he didn't stop, he just went to work.

"What do I do when I get in there?" I whispered but my voice just didn't sound quiet enough.

"Since you are familiar with Gains and Miller, I want you to find anything you can that looks familiar with them. Something we can follow." I nodded, afraid to speak again.

I heard the first lock disengage and Hank went to work on lock number two. My palms started sweating, and I could see a sheen of sweat on Hank's forehead. I started to remember all my encounters with Captain Miller but tried to think of them in a different light and remember details that might lead me in a different direction. I was frustrated because I was always so unconcerned about what was going on around me, I was a 'mind-your-own-business' sort of person.

I had lost myself in thought and the sound of the last lock disengaging drew me from my memories. My eyes widened and I couldn't help feeling fear. Major Jackson took my hands.

"If we need to get out, we get out. Most important is we get that door shut and locked. You will pretend to need him and that you came in here looking for him. I will cut the video thread to start and end with you standing at this door, understand?"

I nodded my head, unable to find my voice, and Hank turned the handle. The air that came out of that room was so cold. I took a deep breath and ducked through the three-lock door.

My mind instantly went into stealth mode. I tried to intently focus on everything around me, the room was neat and tidy, I almost didn't know where to start. There were several filing cabinets along the back wall, all adorned with silver locks. I knew not to waste my time with those, not this time. I saw a cabinet in the back corner without any visible locks, so I started there. The door opened and it was full of uniforms, oddly enough not just US uniforms; there were a few I didn't recognize but I definitely recognized two, from China and Russia. My heart sank and my stomach turned. I was afraid this went much deeper than anyone wanted to believe.

Instantly nausea overtook me. No, no, not now. I was going to puke. I looked everywhere for a garbage can but there was not one in sight. It was coming, that lump in my throat was working its way up and I couldn't do anything about it. I shot for under the desk and there it was. There was an empty drink container right on top. I pried open the lid and held it to my mouth and up it came. I knelt on the floor holding my stomach for a moment. Too long, I was taking too long. I went to stand up when I noticed something from the corner of my eye sticking out to me in the garbage can. A photo. I pulled it from the crinkled papers and gum wrappers.

My stomach turned again; I wasn't sure if I was going to throw up again, so I kept my cup at the ready. I stared incredulously at the photo in my hands. It had four men in it, and three of them I knew all too well. It was old, probably twenty years old, but I knew those faces from anywhere. Colonel Weaver, Sergeant Gains, and Captain Miller. My only reaction was to put my hand to my face in disbelief when the door flew open and Major Jackson was there.

"We have to go, now!" He looked panicked.

I replaced the garbage, put the lid on my puke cup and buried it at the bottom of the trash can. The picture! I shoved it down my pants into the waistband of my underpants and left the room.

I stood in the foyer, my head spinning, my palms sweating, my breathing was becoming uneven. Oh no, I thought again. I was going to pass out. I watched as Major Jackson locked the doors with his little tool, it went a lot quicker than when he unlocked the doors. Once he finished, he looked at me, grabbed my shoulders and positioned me right in front of the door. "Knock!" he said. I reached my hand up and knocked solidly three times before my knees buckled and black closed in.

I awoke to a cold compress on my face. I blinked several times to see a female Asian nurse seated on my bed above me. She was very pretty and feminine looking, but she smiled a forced, tight-lipped smile.

"I understand you weren't feeling well and went looking for Colonel Weaver?" she asked.

I nodded my head, trying to appear weak.

"Well, if you need medical attention, next time come to me," she said in a tone that seemed like she was annoyed with me.

"I'm sorry," I said quietly. "I didn't know what to do."

"And where was your handler?" she asked, while ringing out the towel.

"I insisted that I see Colonel Weaver, he informed me that it was my funeral but took me down anyway."

I had to think of a realistic scenario if we were to be believable and I knew somehow Hank was close and had heard what I said.

Just then, echoing my thoughts, he walked in.

"Thank you, nurse ..." He let it lie, I assumed trying to coax a name out of her. She stood, collected her things, and walked in a huff to her cart by the door.

"Thank you, Major," she said, returning the items to the cart. "But I have a few more questions for Major Giles, please excuse us."

"It's okay," I said. "He can stay."

The nurse shot me a glare.

"No, ma'am, he cannot." Her tone was full of irritation. I guessed this lady didn't like being woken up in the early morning hours. She was definitely on Colonel Weaver's payroll.

Hank left, closing the door behind him. The nurse, whose name I still didn't know, continued with some questioning.

"When did you become ill?"

"I just woke up not feeling right. I didn't get your name?"

"That's because I didn't say it. When and what was the last thing you ate?"

"Dinner, around seven o'clock. I'd like to know who to give credit to."

"It is not your concern. When was your last period?"

It hit me, a roadblock. I had to think. My last period was when I was in the hospital recovering from a broken jaw over a month ago. Oh no. I lied.

"Two weeks ago." It sounded more like a question, even though I didn't believe the sound of my voice.

The nurse glanced up over her clipboard, eyeing me.

"Two weeks ago, you say?" she said.

I couldn't lie with any confidence, and I knew, I knew in the depths of my soul. I swear I could feel the presence inside me, as if I had known it was there all along, and I fought the urge to place my hand over my belly.

"It has been a crazy few weeks, nurse no-name. I can't really be sure, but I would like to get some sleep."

She said nothing, but made some sort of noise under her breath, then she stood and walked very calculatedly to the door.

"I will be sure to pass this along to Colonel Weaver, but don't expect too much sympathy." She shut the door a little too hard and then I knew I was right, she was one of Colonel Weaver's groupies, and she was jealous.

I rushed to the bathroom and looked in the mirror, pulling up my shirt to expose my belly. I knew there was nothing to see but my hand instinctively went there, and I loved it, and would do anything to protect it. All the signs were there, the hormones, the tender breasts, and now the sickness. It seemed strange, now I knew, that I hadn't realized before, everything had shifted with a single question, everything would be different from this moment until forever. And in that same moment, I remembered something else, I stuck my hand into my underwear and felt the photo still where I had placed it.

I pulled it out, revealing again the four boys in the photo. I stared for a moment at Captain Miller's young face, his huge smile. He stood next to Colonel Weaver, their arms around each other's shoulders in a friendly embrace. All four boys were shirtless, and their hair clumped in small spikes from water. I ran my finger over Captain Miller's face and wondered if he could love this baby as I did, or if he would turn away from me. I knew that no matter how bad I wanted it to be William, Colonel Weaver was the father. Weaver used to be his friend, it was obvious from this photo, so what had happened to them? And who was the fourth boy? I had a mission, but my digging in Colonel Weaver's office had taken me in a direction I had never expected to go.

I had seen Major Jackson walk into the room. He came up to me. I had the photo in one hand and my other hand still placed over my belly. I couldn't bring myself to leave the thought I was in.

"Are you okay?" he asked.

I closed my eyes and a soft smile played on my lips and floated up to my eyes.

"Yes, Major Jackson. I am okay!"

I turned to face him and handed him the photo.

"I found that in the garbage, three of them are William

Miller, Jason Weaver, and Sidney Gains. I am not sure who the fourth boy is," I said, pointing out each one.

"This is something," he said. "I am just not sure where to go from here."

"So, it seems we have information without direction," I said, walking out into the room.

"Hey, can I get some crackers, or toast?" I asked, rubbing my belly, at best he would think I had a stomach ache.

"Of course." He walked over to my phone to call down to the kitchen.

I waited while he spoke, ordering me crackers and toast. I didn't know if I wanted to tell him the truth.

"There was something else," I said, waiting for his eye contact.

Honestly, I wasn't sure why Hank had taken me to talk behind a waterfall before but seemed okay to talk now in my room.

"Is it safe?" I asked quietly.

"Who knows?" he said, shaking his head. "I don't know anything anymore, but I have a feeling that things are coming to an end here one way or another. I just want it to be over."

He sounded defeated, I felt bad for him. But he was right, Colonel Weaver was locked down too tight, it would take a literal army, or professionally trained people, to do this.

"There were uniforms, China and Russia, plus a few I didn't recognize. Why would he have them?"

"Not for any good reason, that's for sure. I'll have to

change my report from this afternoon, keep your fingers crossed we make it that far. I might not see you for the rest of the day, just so you know."

"Aww!" I said in a teasing tone. "Will you miss me?"

He stood and closed the distance between us. I flinched back a little because he did it so quickly. He looked at me, and before I knew it he pulled me close to him by my waist, and pressed his lips to mine firmly. I wasn't sure how to react at first, I just stood there motionless and let him kiss me. I don't know if instinct kicked in, where you just kiss someone back because they are kissing you, or that I missed physical affection something terrible, or that the fact that over these last few weeks I had developed feelings for Major Jackson, but I wrapped my arms around his neck and the kiss deepened. He parted my lips with his tongue and his hand moved down, tightly grasping by buttocks. He pulled away as quickly as he had come, staring back and forth between my eyes.

"Take care of yourself," he said, in a serious tone and then added, with a wink, "princess!"

He turned quickly and walked out of the room just as the kitchen brought up my food. I sat at my table, nibbling crackers and poring over all the details that had come to light in just a few hours. I placed my hand over my belly and spoke to the little nugget residing there.

"Well, baby. There is no rest for the weary, or the wicked."

Chapter 19
Fear and Loathing

It felt as though I had just fallen asleep when my door opened with a bang. I jumped and pulled my pillow over my head.

"Jeez, Hank, are you trying to scare me to death?" I asked with a groan.

"Get up, Major Giles," a deep voice said. "Colonel Weaver is waiting."

This was not a voice I recognized. Without taking the pillow away from my face, my eyes shot open. The events from the early morning hours played again in my head in a single second. I wished I had the feeling that we were thorough, that we had been stealthy and were secure. But I was just a pawn in all of this, I had no idea where the plan had come from, nor who was running this show. For all I knew. Major Jackson had set me up and had been on Colonel Weaver's payroll the whole time. I suddenly felt terrified that I had trusted the wrong person. I realized that I was still alone, very alone.

"Major Giles?" the voice boomed, reminding me that I hadn't moved.

"Yes, I'm up. Give me a minute, would you?" I said, pulling the pillow off my face to look my rude alarm clock in the face. He was a tall black man; his shoulders were broad, almost as wide as a door frame. Next, I noticed his deep gold eyes. His skin was very dark and smooth, he sported a high and tight army-style haircut. His gaze wasn't quite cold but fierce, and I wondered if he was one of those guys that looked fierce but was really a teddy bear. I thought better of assumptions, I was not taking any chances and complied without any more hesitation.

He stood by the door, facing me with his arms folded. I walked to my dresser and grabbed a pair of black stretch pants and headed for the bathroom.

"No," he said, "in here."

Where did he think I was going to go? I wasn't sure what was going on but everything about his tone told me that things were bad. Colonel Weaver knew. He knew. I stood awkwardly removing my pajama bottoms, sliding the waist band down until they fell to the floor. I tried to quickly pull the stretch pants on, fumbling everywhere. Why is it when you are trying to hurry everything that can go wrong will go wrong? I wouldn't have blamed him if my new security guard had started laughing at my clumsy display, but he stood unmoving and unamused.

I went to my closet and grabbed a zip-up hoodie and slipped my feet into some simple flip-flops. Pulling my jacket on, I walked toward my door.

"I'm ready," I said, gesturing to myself as though he might have questioned my appearance. My hair was in a loose ponytail with stray hairs dancing around my face. My security guard gave me a disapproving glance when suddenly my stomach turned. My brow furrowed and I made a break for it. I sensed the soldier right on my heels. He probably thought I was going to run.

I rounded the corner, grabbing onto the door frame of the bathroom, and launched myself toward the toilet. He missed me in his grasp as I fell to my knees. I placed my hands on either side of the toilet and vomited. I had all but forgotten about the news I had gotten such a short time ago. As I rested my head against the cold porcelain, I remembered I was not alone.

"Sorry you had to see that," I said, wiping my mouth with the back of my hand. "I might need some crackers … I haven't been feeling well."

His eyes narrowed as he looked at me hunched on the floor.

"You have five minutes to pull yourself together," he said, closing the door behind him. There is nothing more terrifying than being in a situation where you fear for everything and know nothing. To feel completely hopeless and trapped. I felt all those things at once. I now knew exactly what people meant when they said, "My nerves are shot." I walked to the sink and scrubbed my teeth, then paused with the toothbrush hanging out of my mouth while I yanked a brush through my hair. I found myself grateful for those five minutes.

I walked next to my armed guard down the hallway, my

heart pounding in my ears. I could feel my palms getting clammy. With my crackers in hand I tried to organize my thoughts to give myself something else to focus on. I knew I was going to have to play a part, I just had to figure out what part. Who was I? I had never felt so unprepared in my life. Just then, we took a turn into a hallway I had never walked down before. I could see a door at the end, it was a metal door, and I knew it led outside. We exited the house onto a small metal platform; there were stairs leading down to a large grassy area. As we approached the bottom, a man on a golf cart drove up, an American soldier. I didn't know his name, but I had seen him escort Colonel Weaver before. He nodded to my guard, then got out of the driver's seat to let him drive. He hopped on the back, letting me have the other front seat.

"Where are we going?" I asked, trying to seem light-hearted and curious.

No one said a word or even acknowledged that I had spoken. I wasn't sure which was more awkward, to keep silent or ask again. I kept silent. The wind whipped through the cab, blowing my neatly combed hair back to stray hairs everywhere. We kept driving up a dirt road around the mountain. I could see a white building in the distance and beyond that what looked like a stadium or amphitheater. I squinted, trying to make out any detail that I could. As we approached, I noticed a worn red cross on the white building, barely visible. I guessed it was an old hospital, it had to have been long since deserted or I would have known about it. Then again, I wasn't sure of what I did or didn't know anymore.

I became aware of the tires on the rocks, they seemed so loud all of the sudden. I figured whoever was waiting for me knew I had arrived. I felt annoyed that they were so prepared for me, and I was just a pawn in their game. I was supposed to have the upper hand, I was supposed to have an ace up my sleeve. I had nothing. The golf cart came to a halt in front of the old medical building. I slowly slid off the seat. As soon as my feet hit the rock pathway, I had that feeling you get as a child when you want your mom, no one else, just your mom. I was scared, completely scared, there was no room for any other emotion.

My guard quickly came to my side and took my arm. I was grateful because I thought I might need his help to steady my feet. He guided me to a door and leaned in for a retina scan. The door slid open and a gust of air hit me in the face. The air was old and stale and smelled of wet cement and rust, or was it blood? There was a small table with a chair on either side to my right, and a huge mirror that ran the entire wall. Directly in front of me there was a medical-style table with a few tools scattered on it, and a machine with wires and a screen next to it. My guard guided me toward the table when movement caught my eye. Out of a doorway at the other end of the room two men walked through. My mouth dropped open.

Colonel Weaver took Doctor Forrester by the arm and shoved him through the door, he stumbled a couple of steps and then walked toward me. He said nothing, just gestured to me to get on the table. I hopped up and looked at the machine properly for the first time. Oh my gosh, I thought. It was an ultrasound machine.

"Go ahead and lie back, Presley," Doctor Forrester said, "and pull up your shirt a bit for me."

I shot Colonel Weaver a disparaging glance before complying with Doctor Forrester. It wasn't his fault; he was obviously here under duress. I laid back and pulled up my shirt. I was so full of mixed emotions; I knew what was happening and I was both terrified and thrilled to find out if what I already believed was real; up until this point it really was just speculation. But how in the hell did Colonel Weaver know? Or did he just assume based solely on timeline?

Doctor Forrester put a cold gel on my skin, took an instrument from the table, and pressed it to my belly, moving it around a bit. After a few seconds, I heard the erratic whirr of a heartbeat. As much as I hated to share this moment with these people, my captors, the enemy, I couldn't help but smile. I looked at the little bean on the screen and wanted to touch it and say hello, but instead I closed my eyes and thanked God, then asked him for strength.

The moment was over as quickly as it had begun. Doctor Forrester quickly walked over to Colonel Weaver and whispered in his ear. They had a brief conversation, too quiet for me to hear. My guard took Doctor Forrester by the arm and escorted him through the door he had previously come through. Before I could even process what had just happened, a new fear ran through me. I had the sickening thought that Colonel Weaver might want to kill this baby. Instinctively, my hands wrapped tightly around my belly.

"Get up and join me." Colonel Weaver boomed behind me. He walked past me and sat in the chair at the table, the one closest to the door. "It's not a request, Major."

I slid off the table and walked to the colonel, pulled out the chair and sat down. I had no words; I also had the distinct feeling that it would be much better to only speak when spoken to. I placed my hands in my lap and stared at my captor head on. A very strange and sly smile set across his face, I had never seen it before, and I couldn't attach an emotion to it.

"So, what's your theory?" he asked, clasping his hands in front of him on the table.

"On?" I asked, not hiding the annoyance in my voice.

He laughed a harsh, forced laugh.

"Stop, Presley, I am tired of the games. I know you and that sub-human leech Jackson were in my office, I know you took my photo, there is no point giving you a play-by-play, let's just say, I know everything." He stood and leaned forward, placing his hands on the table. "Stop playing games," he said sternly. "What. Are. Your. Theories?" He spoke slowly, as though it would help me understand his request.

"Well, obviously you were childhood friends." Just as I finished my sentence, the door slid open and a gust of hot air flooded in. A man walked through the door and whispered in Colonel Weaver's ear. I didn't need to see his face; I recognized his stature and his walk. Sidney Gains had just walked back into my life. I couldn't think of anyone I wanted to see less than Colonel Weaver; I guess I was wrong.

Sidney jumped back in mock surprise.

"*Doc!*" he shouted as though we were old friends "Fancy meeting you here, how the hell are ya? I hear knocked up?" He shot me a wink-face and handguns then made an obscene gesture with his crotch. I folded my arms over my belly, trying to put some separation between him and anything to do with me. "I wish I could have been there," he said, humping the air.

"Shut up, Sid," Colonel Weaver said, sitting back in his chair. Sidney put both hands up as though he was surrendering and backed up. "So, friends, huh? That's the best you've got. You're dumber than I thought for a smart chick." Weaver leaned his chair back onto its legs and rocked back and forth, studying me. I still felt as though not speaking at all spoke more than anything I had to say. "You're lucky, you know, and you better pray that Forrester is right, or I'll kill you both."

"Right about what?" I asked, genuinely curious.

"The timeline, that baby is mine and the only thing keeping you alive, currently. I might give you time to prove yourself."

I felt the bile in my stomach rise, my hatred for him hadn't changed regardless of whether the little human inside me was half-him; we aren't born bad, evil is a learned behavior. The question that came to my mind then was probably the worst question I could have asked, or perhaps the best.

"So, what are your theories?" I asked, mocking everything about this situation. He laughed, a genuine laugh this time, and his chair crashed back down to all four legs. He slammed his hands on the table, making me jump.

Just then Sidney reappeared from the shadows and whispered once again in Colonel Weaver's ear, who then stood and stared at me.

"He's not my friend, Presley ..." he paused, "he's my brother."

I swallowed hard, trying to grasp the situation. If Sidney Gains was his brother, his dedication to Colonel Weaver made more sense. He interrupted my thoughts.

"If you really want to shit your pants, I'll just come right out with it. You will never see freedom again anyway; trust isn't even an issue, you're mine."

His words were so deep, I think he truly believed I belonged to him.

"He always had everything, the grades, the dad that stuck around, and when he saw you at registration, I saw the look on his face, I saw the way he looked at you—"

I started to interject.

"No!" he yelled. "Shut up, you wanted to know, now shut the hell up and I will tell you."

A vein was protruding in his forehead and his face was red with anger.

"I swore I would outrank him in everything he did, the funny part was, it wasn't even hard. He was always so hung up on doing the right thing, no man left behind and all that. He had to stick his nose in my business, he had to follow me that day."

His emotions betrayed him only for a moment, but I caught it, I saw the pain hiding there.

"I discovered him quickly. See, I know him, I know every trick and every ploy. I would have killed him but instead I sent him off to you, as it were." He laughed and stood, squeezing the bridge of his nose. "I thought it would be greater than any torture I could have dished out, sending him off to be mind-screwed by you, you of all people. I should have just killed him; I will never be that weak again."

I looked back and forth between him and Sidney. I thought his words might have made him feel threatened, but he didn't flinch or budge. Colonel Weaver followed my gaze and read my thoughts and he laughed that booming, forced laugh, it was frightening and sent fear up my spine.

"So, tell me, Major," he sat back down and leaned in to me across the table, I couldn't help but follow his movement and lean away "is it mine?" he asked, then just waited with his hands clasped in front of him. After a few seconds his finger began tapping, showing his impatience.

My eyes burned with tears, I was confused and yet knew exactly what was happening. I was scared and yet all I could say was, "Who else?" I squeezed my eyes shut briefly, holding back the tears, trying desperately not to crack my facade.

Colonel Weaver motioned to Sidney, who flicked a switch and the mirrored wall next to me suddenly turned into a window. There was a white room with a drain in the middle of the floor. A bloodied man was shirtless and tied to a chair, his dark hair hung damp over his brow. My heart clenched and I fought to keep my cool, every atom in my body was screaming to run to him, to cry out to him. I fought it with every ounce of my being. I shifted restlessly in my chair and settled by folding my arms across my chest. My eyes darted back to Colonel Weaver who had a crooked, smile on his face.

"My brother's, of course," he said, in a condescending and matter-of-fact tone. My face shifted ever so slightly back to Captain Miller tied in the chair. It was only for a second, but I knew my emotions were written all over my face. The dawning recognition, the *aha* moment.

"Ahh," he said. "There it is, the pieces are all coming together." He clapped his hands slowly as though to congratulate me.

It's something you wouldn't notice until you knew but they had the same shaped eyes, different colors but the exact same shape, and that strong jawline. I hated myself for being so wrong, and for not seeing it before. Captain Miller was unequivocally Colonel Weaver's half-brother, and I was most definitely stuck between a rock and a very hard place.

Chapter 20
What Now?

Colonel Weaver seemed to be on a high. He was gloating, his jaw slightly lifted, the arrogant tone in his voice. I have to admit, I felt stupid and defeated, I couldn't believe that I hadn't seen all the pieces. I tried to remind myself that I was a person who tried to see the good in people. I wasn't looking for a plot. Colonel Weaver said that Captain Miller had noticed me at registration, I was oblivious to him until he fell into my life, battered, bruised, and bloody, and thus we had come full circle. My new addition had saved me from things I could not imagine at the hands of Colonel Weaver. Since I was already in boiling water, I might as well turn up the heat.

"Why would you send him to me as a punishment?" I asked.

I am sure he could tell I was sincere in asking. I knew

he heard the hurt in my voice, and I made no point in hiding the fact that I was offended. What did I have to lose?

"Ah, did I hurt Doctor Giles's feelings? You see, I told him if he spoke a single word that I would kill you and our whore mother." He laughed. "Then she up and died and all that was left was you. I knew he had to finally be in your presence for it to work, he had to fall for you again and again, and I knew he would, he's so predictable and pathetic. It made sense for his sentence to not be able to speak a word, you see, he never had the courage to ask you out or even say hello. He would just watch you from a distance. I saw his sideways glances, or when he held his breath as you walked by. It's disgusting; even so, I took you before he ever had the chance, and he had to watch it happen."

He paused with a smirk on his face as though he was reminiscing and taking delight in his torture.

"Any other questions?"

I had plenty of questions, but none of which I wanted to hear his answer to.

"Was this planned?" I asked, gesturing to my belly.

"That, well that was a delightful mishap. Don't worry, I won't hurt you while my child grows inside of you, and if you're really good, I might let you help raise it. And I use the word 'help' lightly. I mean you can play happy little housewife and take care of us, how I desire, or you can die."

I knew better than to question him, I knew he believed and meant every word. He was pacing now, every time

223

he turned his back to me my eyes shot to Captain Miller, unmoving and covered in dried blood, sitting in the next room. My muscles twitched, wanting so badly to run to him. His presence was tangible to me, I wondered if he could feel me here.

Colonel Weaver continued: "If it is a boy Ezekiel, a girl, Sarah. 'For God gave us spirit not of fear but of power and love and self-control.' You see, to keep my brother alive took self-control, because at one point I thought I loved him, but love does not last therefore cannot come before power. I desired power, so I took it."

While he was quoting Bible verses, I thought of another question.

"What happened to Hank Jackson?" I let him hear the disdain in my voice; I had learned in his ranting that he wouldn't hurt me. Just as I was starting to believe that he wouldn't, he quickly closed the distance between us and slapped me hard across the face. My head jerked to the side and my hand went up to my cheek. I wasn't going to let him get to me, I wouldn't fall apart. I looked at him once more.

"Well?" I asked.

"Where was that fight when I was holding you down?" he asked.

I fought the urge to spit on him. I couldn't believe how much I hated this man; I didn't know this type of feeling existed inside of me.

"He will join my brother in the ring."

"The ring?" I asked, it sounded even more asinine coming out of my mouth, it sounded like something from a bad thriller movie.

His face turned into something evil and disturbing.

"The execution ring … *princess.*"

The emphasis on the word princess sent chills up my spine. I knew he knew about me and Major Jackson, he knew everything. I felt like throwing up, not pregnancy throwing up but disgusting gut-churning, acid-rising, hands-on-the-knees-type of throwing up.

Out of nowhere, two men entered the room that Captain Miller was in, unshackled him and dragged him out. Suddenly, the words *execution ring* seemed more ominous and impending than they had moments ago when I thought it was an exaggeration. Then, one of the men standing by the door whispered in Colonel Weaver's ear. A smile played across his face from ear to ear. A real fear had risen inside me, I found myself searching for an out, any place that was safe. I stared at the floor, letting my eyes lose focus. My hearing blurred out as well. I heard commotion and somewhere in my senses I could feel movement all around me.

I was jolted back into my nightmare when someone touched me.

"Major Giles, I'm Sisi. I am going to be your stylist for today."

Sisi was plain, medium build, medium height, with medium brown hair, not someone I would expect to call herself a stylist. My first thought: Why do I need a stylist?

She ushered me through a door at the back of the room; I hadn't even noticed it there before. Inside was a white desk with a round mirror and lights surrounding it, like you would imagine in a Hollywood dressing room. There was a rack on one wall with lots of clothes on it, most of them seemed more of the party variety, fancier than I was used to. Where was I going? No thought was pleasant. She guided me over to the chair in front of the lighted mirror. My reflection was gaunt and tired-looking. My hair was in a ponytail with flyaway hair around my face. I didn't know the person who was looking back at me.

Here in this room, just Sisi and I, I felt the facade start to melt away. Tears burned in my eyes, and I was becoming increasingly unable to keep them from spilling over. The last few months of my life were playing repeatedly in my head at warp speed. It was an emotional roller coaster that was starting to make me motion sick. I lay my head down on the desk and let the tears come. To my surprise, Sisi put her arm around me to comfort me. She seemed less and less like someone who would be willingly hanging out with Colonel Weaver. I felt heavy with all the many emotions that were catching up with me from weeks and weeks of confusion.

I sat there in a blur, not seeing anything, not hearing anything, only mildly aware that someone was pulling and brushing my hair. I had heard that in near-death experiences, your life can pass before your eyes. Was I dying? Because that was what was happening. I remembered when I was a little girl sitting in front of a mirror while my mother brushed and pulled my hair into a tight ponytail. But this was not the same, I didn't feel loved or like I was being taken care of; I felt like I was being handled. I didn't feel any hostility from Sisi, just that she was simply doing her job, and I was certain she was nothing more than an employee. I have to admit there was something about her that made everything else seem like a dream and that I was just at the salon getting my hair done. I was grateful for her.

Regardless of her part in all of this, I knew what was out there waiting if I was to stick one toe out of line: some kind of trapdoor spider waiting to pounce on its prey. I sat in silence and let her hands flit about my hair and face. I didn't have a game plan, I needed to wait for the enemy to make another move and hoped that when the time came, I would know what to do. My biggest problem was that I didn't know who was a friend and who was foe. I was dragged out of my silence by someone clearing their throat. I turned to see Sisi standing behind me, holding up a dress. It was all black, satin, with a scoop neck and thin metal straps that crossed in the back and plunged all the way down to the waist.

"Well?" Sisi asked, giving the dress a jiggle on its hanger. "What do you think?"

I paused and gave her a tight-lipped smile.

"Looks like a party." I couldn't hide my snarky tone, and didn't really want to, I was done acting, I was done faking it. Whatever was coming for me was going to have to come. Without taking the time to appreciate Sisi's hard work, I stood and walked over to her. She helped me slip the dress over my head, making sure to protect her masterpiece. The dress slipped over my body and fell in a black curtain around me. The fabric was so thin I felt naked. I was afraid to move for fear that the fabric would tear at the seams. I fidgeted with the neckline trying to figure out just how it was supposed to lay when I caught Sisi staring. Did she have tears in her eyes?

"Are you okay?" I asked.

"You just look so beautiful. The Colonel is such a lucky man, and you, miss, are a very lucky woman." She was standing next to me now, with her hands on my shoulders, as she turned my body to face the mirror.

She was joking, right? She had no clue about the monster she worked for; ignorance is bliss when it comes to these things. I let myself focus on the reflection. Under different circumstances I would have felt beautiful, I would have been looking forward to whatever awaited me out that door. Such as it was, I was horrified and the fact that I was being dressed up and paraded around scared me even more.

"Let's get you to that party then, miss," she said. Her cadence was like something from 1940's New York, a Brooklyn girl from the old movies. I did not feel like taking my anger out on this girl who seemed sweet and kind, even if only in that moment.

"Lead the way!" I said, taking her arm as though she was my date. As we walked back out into the white room, the first thing I noticed was the empty chair that had once held Captain Miller. My heart sped up and my mind jumped all over. I was no longer scared for myself but terrified for him.

Chapter 21

Fight or Flight

As Sisi opened the door, sunlight flooded in, blinding me. I put my hand up to shield my eyes. The air was thick and tasted like damp dirt, there wasn't a cloud to be seen but I could feel the pressure, I could feel the weather that was coming. I could hear a buzz in the distance, like one hundred people whispering all at once. As my eyes focused, I could see a hundred feet ahead of us there was a procession of soldiers being led through some doors, they were all dirty to varying degrees and their hands were tied with something behind their backs. I recognized the third from the back was Major Jackson; I knew it as soon as I saw him. I realized it with a sense of relief because if he was there, then it meant he was truly on my side and for that I was grateful. It was becoming more and more important that I figured out a way to save not only myself but Captain Miller and Major Jackson as well.

Before I could have even decided to make a run for it, in my black satin dress and stiletto heels, there were three soldiers at my side with guns. I laughed jeeringly.

"All of this for little old me? I must be super-important."

One of the soldiers stepped in front of me. I had seen him before. He towered above me, dark, silky skin. I tried to make eye contact, but he was so tall that the sun inhibited my view. He took one step to the right blocking the sun from my eyes.

"Follow me ..." he trailed off, " ... princess."

I squinted up at him, making a face I couldn't hide, and my heart skipped a beat. He called me princess, but not in the way Colonel Weaver had said it. He said it the way Major Jackson always said it. I had to wonder if it was a hint or if he was just one of the many people I had recently encountered that seemed to enjoy annoying me. I couldn't ignore it and yet I couldn't count on it either. I told myself once again to be ready for anything. I took a deep breath and inwardly told myself, "here we go." I took a step forward and immediately stumbled; the soldier to my left caught my arm.

"I'm good, I'm good," I reassured them, putting up both of my hands as if to surrender. I grabbed the hem of my dress and held it up in true princess fashion and followed the dark soldier through the trees ahead of me; I felt like I was walking toward something ominous. I could feel it, and it wasn't the weather, this was something else entirely.

As we cleared the trees, I could see now what I had been hearing. A large crowd had gathered and was seated in something along the lines of an arena or a stadium. Half of it had stone walls carved into the side of a mountain and felt like Ancient Rome; the other side was more like high school bleachers. In the middle were four large stones that gave me a Stonehenge vibe. The stones had two chains with cuffs hanging down on either side. As I followed the soldiers into the clearing, I saw the prisoner soldiers being led over to the stones. As they were cuffing them, I spotted Captain Miller. He seemed completely out of it, barely conscious, two soldiers had to drag him over to the stones. Once he was locked in, they pulled the chain so that his arms were stretched above his head. His knees were buckled, and he was just hanging there. In my watching I hadn't noticed that the soldier in front of me had stopped, if it hadn't been for the soldier next to me grabbing hold of my arm, I would have walked right into him. He leaned down with a tight grip on my arm and angrily whispered into my ear: "See something you like?" His mouth turned up on one side in a lopsided smile.

I tried to free my arm from his grasp, but he held tighter. Our eyes met, each with an emotion toward each other that could only be called disdain. I hated this man, and I didn't even know his name.

"Stay tuned, things are going to get good."

Just then, the tall, dark soldier in the front turned and looked at my captor dead on, the look in his eyes would have stopped a bear in its tracks.

"I will take her from here," he said in his deep voice.

If he had been talking to me, I might have done anything he asked me to. He gripped my other arm and pulled me from the other soldier's grasp. I didn't feel like a human anymore, just a shiny object that both men wanted to control. We walked into the arena, my eyes darting everywhere, trying to take it all in, trying desperately to locate an out, anything. In my searching, my eyes caught Major Jackson being shackled on the other side of the stones. As they pulled the chain to raise his arms he spat in the face of the guard. I couldn't help but smile, at least he was upright on his own accord. The smile was immediately erased when the soldier punched him in the stomach, wiping the smirk off Major Jackson's face. I cringed and kept walking. We came to a set of stairs that led up to a stone box with two red, throne-like chairs. I noticed who was seated in one of the chairs and it was obvious that he thought of himself as a king. I shuddered to think that the one to his left was for me, but I was not his queen, just a slave to his desires, and a servant to his needs.

As I ascended the stairs, Colonel Weaver made eye contact with me, entire conversations passed between us, months of forced moments and secret glances were put out there, floating in the air like pollution. We were on the same page, but in two different books, the only common place was hatred. We both knew the storm was coming, and echoing my thoughts, a gust of wind came through the arena, cold and biting, unnatural for this place. I wrapped my arms around myself. I knew as I watched him watching me, that I would fight. I moved my hands to my belly as if to protect the little bean inside me. I watched Colonel Weaver smile that crooked, slimy smile

I had grown to despise. He thought he had me by the proverbial balls, he thought he had me pegged, but there was a new bear that had awoken inside me, the mama bear, and even I didn't know what to expect from her.

As I reached Colonel Weaver he stood and greeted me with a nod, then placed his hand on the small of my back and guided me to my chair. I sat and leaned into him.

"I see we are still pretending," I said, settling in on my makeshift throne.

"As it seems one of us is better at this pretending thing than the other." Colonel Weaver cut me off by grabbing hold of my arm at the wrist. "I have no problem helping you keep that mouth shut."

Colonel Weaver turned away, then smiled and waved at some men standing across the way. They were wearing a Chinese military uniform. My skin began to crawl, being at war with China and seeing them standing there so comfortably felt so wrong. Just then a man wearing a uniform I had never seen walked up and reached out a hand to Colonel Weaver who stood to greet him. They leaned in and spoke to each other quietly while grasping each other's hands the entire time. I studied the strange embrace; I couldn't tell if it was tension or comradery that kept the men in their embrace. As I rubbed my arm where he had grabbed me, he turned back and stared at me, leaning on the arm of the chair so that no one else could see his face. I wasn't scared really but I also wasn't too eager to see how far I could push him.

"I can handle it, thanks," I said, echoing his tone.

He suddenly wrapped his hand in my hair at the back

of my head and pulled my head to one side, taking me off guard. My breathing increased but I managed to maintain some sort of composure. With his free hand he somehow produced a knife and pressed it to my throat. I was aware of all the people around and watching, a detail that didn't seem to bother him. He leaned in to my ear.

"Do you think I care what any of these people think? Do you think any of them would care if I slit your throat right now? If you are interested in keeping your head attached to your body, I wouldn't test me, Major."

I could feel the sting of the knife's tip and the warm drop of blood running down my chest. I didn't doubt his words and I wished I didn't care, but I did. My original plan to turn up the attitude was going to have to take a back seat. I managed to form words, although my jaw was trembling.

"Okay, I'm sorry ..." I paused. "I'll shut up."

He released my head with a jolt and looked pleased with the way things had gone when we were interrupted by the man I had seen with the Chinese uniform. He approached like he had interrupted a pleasant conversation and nothing else. I tried to smooth down my dress and wipe the blood from my neck and chest and fiddled with my hair, which I was sure he had messed up. I tried to listen to the conversation. Colonel Weaver was a smart man and never ceased to impress. He was speaking fluent Mandarin. While his attention was elsewhere, I looked to the arena. Major Jackson was staring right at me, our eyes met and my heart started to race. I wished that I could be their savior, but I was a prisoner just like them.

I stared down at Major Jackson and tried to portray something like *I'm sorry* on my face. My body instinctively sat forward, Colonel Weaver didn't seem to notice and then I saw it. It was quick but I knew it with every fiber of my being, and I knew it was intentional. Major Jackson winked at me. Suddenly, I was filled with a feeling that threatened to escape my lips. Hope, I was filled with hope.

Chapter 22
Sounds Like Thunder

I started to notice that random groups of people were coming to order. I was anxious for this strange event in my life to start and, hopefully sooner rather than later, come to an end. Colonel Weaver shifted in his seat; I noticed his forehead displaying a fine sheen of sweat. For the first time since I'd known him, he had lost that arrogant confidence; he seemed nervous. I watched as men in different uniforms strolled in from all four corners of the arena and took their seats in groups of their own said uniforms. Colonel Weaver continued in his awkward silence, but he had graduated to resting his forehead on his hand looking like he was nursing a headache, seeming to avoid contact with anyone. I think I preferred his arrogance. My glance kept returning to Captain Miller, who still seemed unconscious, and Major Jackson who seemed calm, I noticed he was speaking, or at least his lips were moving, and it looked as though he was trying to hide it. Just then I saw a guard walk over to him. They seemed to be arguing back and forth, then the guard slammed the butt of his gun into Major Jackson's face.

I couldn't help but flinch, which wouldn't have been a problem except that it drew Colonel Weaver's attention back to me. He reached over and took my hand; had it been any other person I would have felt like it was endearing, but with Colonel Weaver I knew better. His grip got tighter, and he pulled me closer. His eyes met mine for a moment, I tried to read them but there was an onslaught of emotions swimming frantically all at once. His eyes darted back and forth to mine, he took a breath like he was about to say something, paused, then thought better of it and sat back in his chair.

The Chinese man I had seen enter the arena stood and started shouting, there was a translator standing next to him.

"Ānjìng de."

"Quiet!"

I was surprised at how quickly the talking ceased and the attention was all on this short, stocky Chinese man. His translator had a hard time keeping up, but I gathered he was introducing someone. Just then a small group of men walked through the corner of the arena closest to the prisoners. My heart leaped and started pounding instantly. I recognized the leaders of the Chinese and Russian army. Colonel Weaver sat up straighter in his chair and fiddled with his uniform. Soldiers filed in behind them and they made their way toward us. Colonel Weaver stood, pulling me up behind him just as a huge clap of thunder rebounded off the walls of the arena. I jumped, hands on chest, I was aware that Colonel Weaver was watching me. I looked up at him. He had a smirk on his face.

"You handled that well," he said, voice full of ridicule.

I rolled my eyes just as another clap of thunder rolled in. I felt a cold drop on my shoulder, then another. I was so absorbed by everything going on around me, I hadn't noticed the sky had turned gray with thick cloud cover. In the distance I heard more thunder, but it seemed to be getting closer. Before I realized that it was not thunder, a warm hand clapped over my mouth and pulled me down, as a huge explosion sent my hands to my ears. We were under attack. I was too perplexed to even notice who had ahold of me, but I was being pulled toward the front of the arena.

I got my face free enough to look into the eyes of my captor. It was the tall dark soldier who had escorted me here. He pushed a bag into my chest, it was a backpack.

"Climb on. Princess," he said, with a wink.

I glanced behind me briefly to notice Colonel Weaver crouched down speaking into a walkie-talkie. I quickly measured my options, every sense in me went up a couple of notches and I felt I could trust this man. I flung the backpack over my shoulder, kicked off my shoes, and tried to climb on but I couldn't move. My pack was stuck on something. I turned to free myself and noticed it was not something but someone. Sidney Gains had a hold of me, rage on his face.

The dark soldier had turned around and immediately

started going head-to-head with Sidney. I grabbed my pack and got out of their way. I couldn't watch the hand-to-hand combat and crouched down with my eyes closed. I wasn't sure who had won but I heard the noise of the battle stop. My dark soldier stood above me with blood running from his lip. He motioned for me to climb onto his back. I felt like I was perched on the back of a gorilla as he ran toward the prisoners. Bombs continued to go off all around us. I buried my head in his neck, I didn't want to see any of it. I could feel his pace slowing and he shifted, signaling me to get off. My feet slid to the ground with a jolt. I was standing at the stones where Major Jackson was bleeding and fiddling with his restraints. The soldier went to him and unlocked both of his hands.

"Let's go!" Major Jackson yelled to us and several other men standing around. He paused and looked at me. "You good?"

I smiled as best as I could but didn't speak; it was loud and there was gunfire everywhere. I then noticed there were armed soldiers surrounding us, taking aim. He motioned for us to follow him.

"*Wait!*" I yelled and started toward Captain Miller. Major Jackson grabbed my arm. "He is just a war criminal, Presley, let him go." I jerked my arm away and glared into his eyes.

"Well, I'm not leaving without him."

Major Jackson paused briefly then let out a groan and signaled to have him released. The black soldier went to him and pulled him off the stone, he wasn't steady, so he wrapped his arm around his shoulder and pulled him along. A gunshot sounded and I saw them both go down; I watched in horror as they both fell to the ground. Another soldier dragged me out of the arena through some trees. I cried out but my voice was drowned out by the bombs and gunfire. Tears welled in my eyes when I saw them, arm-in-arm, limping through the clearing in the trees.

We all ran together for about a half a mile when we came to what looked like a shipping container and we all filed inside. It was dark and smelled of rust. Empty shipping boxes and metal instruments of some sort littered the floor. Men were seated on boxes and anywhere they could find a spot. The black soldier came through, carrying Captain Miller on his shoulder. He dumped him on the ground with a thud. I could see he was breathing, and I turned to the tall black man who had been my captor, and my savior.

"What is your name, soldier?" I asked, out of breath.

He looked at me and took a couple of shallow breaths.

"Orville," he said. "Most people just call me Villy."

I walked over to him and examined the gunshot wound to his left shoulder; the bullet had gone clean through.

"Captain, Major, Colonel?" I asked, walking around and examining his shoulder. "Just trying to clarify."

"Just Villy," he said.

I walked around to face him and offered him my hand.

"Thank you, Villy, you have my friendship. That is a clean wound but you will need to get it stitched up. I am happy to take care of it when we get to a medical facility."

He shook my hand and gestured toward Captain Miller with his head.

"He's in a bad way, was he worth the trouble?"

Major Jackson walked over to us.

"You get dressed, Presley, I will tend to Captain Miller."

I hesitated, just standing there.

"I promise," he said.

I went to walk away then turned back.

"Get dressed?" I asked.

"The backpack," was all he said as he knelt down to Captain Miller's side.

I took the backpack off and opened it. Inside were some pants, boots, a fitted tank top, and a jacket. I was standing there in a small space with about twelve men, and I was supposed to get dressed. I listened to the sounds around me, the gunfire in the background, and the heavy unsteady breathing of everyone in the shipping container, these men didn't care about anything but their own safety. I took myself over into a corner and faced away from them. I pulled the pants on under my black dress, which was now ripped in several places. I slipped the dress off over my pants and quickly pulled the top on. I turned around to see everyone looking at the same place; I followed their gaze to Captain Miller, who was now awake.

"*Will*!" I called out and fell to my knees by his side. His name sounded foreign on my lips. He looked at me, but it seemed he was looking through me, as though he didn't see me at all.

"Presley, we can't stay here," Major Jackson said, sliding a gun into a holster and one over his shoulder.

I tried to put my emotions in check and stand up, I told my brain to stand but it didn't comply. Major Jackson placed his hand under my arm and helped me to my feet.

"What's wrong with him?" I asked.

"He will come around; I shot him with some pretty serious pain meds. Now hurry, we need to move."

I sat down to put on the boots and realized my feet were sore and bleeding from running barefoot. I pulled the boots on and tied them tightly. I could hear the gunfire still in the distance. Major Jackson motioned for us all to exit the shipping container. Three men filed out before me, and Villy, with Captain Miller still sort of slumped at his side, was behind me. I cautiously followed the men in front of me when a gunshot echoed through my ears, it was close. I tried to turn and see but there were two soldiers at my side who pushed me forward. They pulled me on, through the forest, trees scratching my face and twigs and branches hitting my legs. We finally broke through the trees into a clearing. All the soldiers made a circle and drew their guns, Villy and Captain Miller were in the middle of the circle with me. I was trying desperately to do a headcount when I saw a soldier carrying someone on his back. He entered the circle and placed the man on the ground. He was holding Major Jackson who was covered in blood.

"*No!*" I cried.

I went to his side and tried to find where the bleeding was coming from. I pulled open his jacket and the blood was pooling from his chest. I slapped my hands down and applied pressure, but I knew, I knew even if there were surgical instruments right here, right now, that this was a fatal wound. His chest rose and fell, his breathing already growing more shallow. I could hear the gurgle from his lungs filling with blood.

"Don't leave me," I whispered.

My head dropped but I did not release pressure on his wound. I could feel the warm blood spilling over my fingers, I could feel his breath leaving.

"*No, Hank, no!*" I cried again.

I couldn't let this happen; I couldn't just let him fade away without a fight. I started CPR. With every chest compression the blood escaped and ran down his sides. The tears were running hot down my cheeks, "One, two, three." Villy was next to me on the ground, I didn't know how long he had been there. He put a hand on my shoulder.

"*No,*" I said again. I couldn't give up.

He then took my face in his hands and turned my face to his.

"No," I whispered, searching his eyes for some form of comfort.

"He's gone, Major," Villy said, pulling me into him.

I buried my head in his chest and gripped his jacket in my hands.

"We have to go," he said reluctantly, and pushed me away. He looked back and forth into my eyes. "Be strong now, Major, we must live for his sacrifice."

I looked down at Major Jackson, his chest now still and I watched the light leave his eyes. I leaned down and kissed his forehead, closing his eyes with one hand.

"I will never forget you," I whispered.

" Let's go," I said to Villy, wiping the wetness from my cheeks with my sleeve.

Villy was right, Major Jackson had sacrificed himself

243

for me and I would never let his death be in vain. Villy led the way past the clearing and back into the woods, he had scooped up Captain Miller and they were limping away in front of me. The soldiers filed in behind us. Things started feeling less urgent and I knew we were close to where we were going. I could hear rushing water, and as we rounded a corner, I could see an American flag in the distance. This part of the forest seemed different, like I was somewhere else altogether, there were tall, sprawling pines, and the mountainside was littered with large white rocks that looked like they had rolled into place a thousand years ago. We stopped just before the forest opened into a huge riverbank.

Villy motioned for us to stop and sent two soldiers on ahead. We stood there in silence, a flash of lightning overhead followed by a loud clap of thunder sent the raindrops falling. I had never been caught in a downpour like this; we were instantly soaked. I noticed the soldiers shift to high alert. The rain made it harder to hear what was coming.

"Let's make a run for it, we aren't safe out here like this," Villy said to another soldier.

"We have gimpy here," he answered back.

"I'll take him," Villy said, then made eye contact with me.

I couldn't even look at Captain Miller. I was so confused by this, I thought of nothing else, but this person wasn't him. I was scared to look into his eyes and see that he was no longer there. I feared for what Colonel Weaver had done to him, maybe he would never be the same, maybe he didn't even know who I was and never would, and so I stared at the ground and awaited the go ahead to make a run for it. I was a soldier too, after all.

After just a couple of minutes Villy stood, picked up Captain Miller and flung him over his shoulder like a fireman, and ushered us into the river. It was wide but shallow; we easily walked across. Once we reached the other side, we were greeted by several other soldiers holding an American flag.

"Where is General Jackson?" one of them asked.

"He didn't make it," Villy said.

Wait! General? Hank was a General? I suddenly felt silly at how I had interacted with him. Villy was explaining where to find his body and I wondered what else I didn't know. The man sent Villy and two other soldiers back in the direction we came from, presumably to get General Jackson's body. And then ushered Captain Miller and I to the medical tent.

I could see Captain Miller lying on the table a few feet away. There was a nurse hovering over him hooking up an IV and another taking vials of blood. News must travel fast because a doctored rolled an ultrasound machine over to me.

"How are you?" he asked while he fiddled with some wires. "Can you lie back? My name is Doctor Hillyard." He lifted my shirt and squirted some gel on my belly. That quick little whirr of my baby's heartbeat played like a melody for the room. I smiled and everything else melted away. "The baby sounds good, Major."

"How did you know?" I asked.

"General Jackson mentioned it at our briefing this morning, before allowing himself to get caught," he said with a smirk. "He wanted to make sure we had the necessary equipment, and he didn't know for sure what condition you would be in."

I thought of many things to say, and questions to ask, but just settled for, "Thank you."

"Would you like to know how far along you are?" he asked, moving the monitor around on my belly. "You are just over nine weeks, which is probably why you have had some tummy trouble."

The idea of knowing who the father was had made me nervous. It happened that night with Weaver in his bedroom, timing was against me; I knew who the father was.

My heart started to ache thinking of Hank, knowing that was how doctor Hillyard had gotten all of his information, then my stomach turned when my thoughts returned to Colonel Weaver being the father of my baby, the brother of the man I loved, and the last person I ever wanted to be the father to anyone. The doctor started to clean up the gel on my stomach.

"Wait," I said, sitting up. "Do we know the status of Colonel Weaver?"

"All I know is that he was severely injured and taken into custody. I imagine he will be extradited back to the States for trial."

"Do you think I will have to testify?"

"Don't take my word for it, but I would imagine that you are their star witness with the General being gone."

My eyes dropped and we both offered a moment of silence.

"He was a good man," he said. I nodded in agreement, fearing words would bring tears. He placed his hand on my shoulder, offering a little comfort, and walked away. Now that I knew I was okay, and my baby was okay, I turned my attention to Captain Miller. I took a deep breath and walked toward his bed.

Chapter 23
All Buttoned Up

Before I got to Captain Miller's bed, I was stopped by two soldiers. I didn't even realize they were standing guard.

"Gentlemen, I just want to lend a hand, I am a doctor after all."

"We can't let you near him, Major Giles," one of them said. "He is a war criminal; he cannot be trusted." This was the other.

"He was framed by Colonel Weaver. Trust me, I know …"

"You will have to tell it to a judge, Major," the first one spoke again.

"Please, Captain …?"

"Sikes," he said, "Captain Sikes."

"Please, Captain Sikes, just let me verify that he is okay, you can stand right there with me."

He sighed a heavy sigh and pinched the bridge of his nose.

"Alright, Major, but make it quick."

I walked with Captain Sikes over to Captain Miller's bed. His eyes were open, but I could tell that he wasn't fully there yet. I took Captain Miller's hand; it was cold and clammy. Captain Sikes stepped between us, forcing our hands apart.

"I cannot allow you to touch him, Major. We don't know what is affecting him."

"Alright, I get it," I said stepping back. "What do we know?"

A nurse standing next to me handed me his chart.

"It seems he has been injected with a strong hallucinogen, we are running tests so that we know how to counter the effects."

She pointed out some check marks to me and flipped over a page to show me his bloodwork. She glanced at the soldier to my left, whose name I didn't get but was a Major, like me. He nodded and she turned one more page. There was a list of possible hallucinogens.

I studied the notes and the body scan that they had just finished taking. He had a concussion and a fractured wrist and nose, a dislocated shoulder and a severely damaged knee. Not to mention many cuts and bruises.

"Give him a good dose of naloxone, it won't hurt him and if he used ketamine it will help. Colonel Weaver had many animals on his ranch, I could see ketamine being readily available without drawing attention."

The nurse took the chart and thanked me.

"It is time to go, Major Giles," Captain Sikes said, gesturing with his hand as if to show me the way.

"Now where am I going?" I asked, confused.

"There is a chopper waiting to take you to the airfield, we need to get you back to the States for debriefing."

I knew better than to resist or ask questions but figured that since I was a hot commodity, maybe I had some pull.

"I am not going unless I can ensure that I am kept in the loop about Captain Miller, when and where he goes."

"Of course," Captain Sikes said.

"That easy, huh? Just an 'of course' without having to ask anyone ... Captain?" I knew I was being condescending, but I needed to know I could count on him.

He looked at the Major who had been escorting us. He stepped away with a walkie-talkie pressed to his lips. He came back over to us, nodded, and said with a snide tone, "Of course, Major Giles."

I briefly broke free and leaned down to Captain Miller. I told him, "I will come back for you." And just before they pulled me away, I whispered, "I love you."

Before I knew it, I was loaded onto a helicopter and heading back to the United States. I hadn't been home in eight years; I was just a kid when I landed here, I finished school and did my residency here. I only wished I had something or someone to go home to.

"Major, Major Giles, we are here."

Great, another voice I didn't recognize, pulling me out of a deep sleep. I willed myself to wake up, it had been a long time since I'd had a good night's sleep.

"Let me help you up, Major, you slept like the dead," she joked.

"I'm sorry," I said clearing the grog out of my throat. "Do I know you?"

"No, Major, we haven't met. I am Tina, your liaison."

"Hi, Tina, nice to meet you." I rubbed my eyes and tried to stand up. "A three-hour flight was not long enough."

"Let's get you to your room."

I was tired and dirty. I remembered that I still had General Jackson's blood on my clothes and probably under my fingernails. A hotel sounded fantastic. When I stepped off the plane onto the tarmac there was a long black car waiting for me. Tina opened the door and offered for me to get in. We drove down the streets of Fort Hood, toward the military base. I could see the huge American flag blowing in the distance. Across from the base were three large white buildings where many of the soldiers stayed. They had good food here; I at least remember that. I was excited for a hot shower and a good meal.

We pulled up and Tina hopped out, holding the door for me. She closed it behind me and said in her bubbly voice, "Follow me!"

I wasn't sure if I envied her happy-go-lucky tone or if I secretly wanted to slap the happy off her face. Either way, I followed without complaint.

My room was simple: a bed, a desk with a chair, and a dresser. The best part was the bathroom with a shower. One thing about Tina, she didn't hover. She got me settled and left me to my own devices. I sat on the floor of the shower, praying the water would wash away many things: feelings, emotions, and blood, especially the blood on my hands. I stared down at my hands, remembering Hank's face, the look of fear and desperation. He knew he was going to die, and my face was the last thing he saw. I wanted to remember him alive, I closed my eyes and remembered him diving into the spring in the mountains, and him irritating me on purpose because he liked to watch me squirm. I would give anything to hear his snarky remarks.

I was interrupted by a knock on my door and Tina's muffled voice.

"Major Giles, there is someone here for you."

A man's voice followed, "No need to stand on ceremony, Major, just get decent and come out here."

The voice was vaguely familiar.

I got out, wrapped my head in a towel and put on the provided bathrobe. I knew nothing good could come from a rushed non-appointment and I opened the door.

General Albrechtson stood in my doorway. He was over my entire department.

"General! Good to see you." I scrambled, trying to salute. He waved a hand my way.

"No need, Major, have a seat."

I walked over to the bed, and he sat across from me in the chair from the desk.

"I have good news and bad news, Major. You don't have to be dragged through a mess of a trial; Colonel Weaver passed away at the hospital just before you got here."

I hesitated, not sure how to feel; part of me felt sadness but it was overtaken by relief. I had never hated anyone like I hated him and yet he was the father of my baby.

"Also, the home in which you resided for eight years is yours if you want it, included as a severance package and an honorable discharge from the army, if you want it."

I wasn't expecting that, none of it. I was speechless.

"Look," he continued, "you have some time to decide, because previously you could only be discharged after a mandatory evaluation; you of all people should know what that entails. We appreciate your service and you helped with our investigation more than you know."

"General, I didn't even know …" I trailed off.

"I know, Major, keeping you in the dark was key to it working. We had an inkling when Sidney Gains was sent to you. He was presumed dead for three years then suddenly popped back up as your patient. General Jackson volunteered to go himself, but he wanted to be on a level playing field with you and went in as Major Jackson. When Captain Miller sent you to the hospital, Hank insisted he be the one to handle this case too."

"Will there be a service?" I asked. "For General Jackson?"

"Yes, a week from Sunday."

"I would like to attend. And what about Captain Miller?"

"Yes, I was notified to keep you in the loop. I was reluctant to do so, but because it is you asking, he will stand trial when he is well enough to do so. I will let you know when I know. Oh, and good job on the naloxone, you hit the nail on the head with that one."

"So, he is okay then?" I asked.

He stood and I stood.

253

"He has a long road ahead of him. Good day, Major, I will send over the complete debriefing for you to look over, unredacted."

"Thank you, General."

And with that he left. Tina came in from the hall with a silver tray, the kind that always had food on it.

Chapter 24
All Good Things

The day was gloomy, overcast but hot and muggy. I smoothed my new black uniform and tucked some stray hairs into my hat. Today I would attend General Jackson's funeral, today I would say goodbye to a friend.

Tina popped her head into the bathroom: "Are you ready?" Before I could answer, she said, "Oh, Presley, I mean Major Giles, you look so regal, so beautiful."

"Thanks, Tina, yes I am ready."

The drive to the cemetery was about fifteen minutes, only family attended the church, so we were headed graveside. As we pulled up, I could see American flags stuck all over in the lawn, and his family, his parents, and I could only guess his brother and sisters, seated all around the grave. I stood as close as I could get, blending in with the rest of the uniforms. I stood with my head down and listened to the rifle detail. The sound of the jets overhead made my heart flutter with sadness and pride. The pastor talked more about General Jackson and I wondered if I was the only person here who knew him in the way that I did. I felt honored to call him a friend. I listened to 'Taps' play and watched as the casket was lowered into the ground. I fought a tear that managed to escape and run down my cheek. As he disappeared into the earth, I made a decision.

After the funeral ended and the people had dispersed, I found the person I was looking for. General Albrechtson stood facing away from me at the other end of the graveside.

"General," I said, tapping his shoulder to get his attention.

"Major Giles, hello."

"I have made my decision. I will take you up on that offer. I'd like to go home and raise my baby."

"I thought you would." He reached out for my hand to shake it.

"As soon as you finish your sessions with Doctor Allen, you are good to go. I will notify him to get the arrangements going."

"Thank you, General. Oh, and any news from Captain Miller?"

His face went ashen as he fumbled around in his pockets.

"Ah, yes, I have this."

He handed me an envelope with an American seal on it. My heart sunk; it was the envelope they sent to fallen soldiers' families to notify them of their death.

"I'm sorry," he said, and quickly walked away.

I opened the letter.

Dear Major Giles,

We have been notified of your request for information on Captain Miller. After he was healthy enough to stand trial, he was moved to a different facility. We could find no other information regarding Captain William Miller and presume him executed for his crimes.

Sincerely,
General Andhers

I crumpled the paper in my hands and dropped it where I stood. I walked over to a flower arrangement and took one rose. I stood at the edge of the grave and dropped it on top of the casket. My hands were shaking, it was hard enough to say goodbye to one friend, I wasn't ready to accept Captain Miller's death.

"Wish me luck, Hank, I am off to a new adventure." I spoke quietly enough that my voice disappeared into the breeze. It was only for us to hear.

I made my way back to my barracks, watching the trees pass me by, stretching like ghosts across the windows. Tina sat up front with the driver, giving me the back seat to myself. I placed my hands on my belly and cried. I cried for my baby's father who I had to believe was once good, tears for the only man I ever truly loved, gone before our story was complete, and a tear for my friend who was there when no one else was, and lastly, a tear for me; for everything I had been through, and then I closed that book and vowed to move forward, to move on.

Luckily for me, my sessions with Doctor Allen went off without a hitch. I knew just what to say and how to say it to get a pass on the clean bill of health. I am sure Doctor Allen knew what I was up to. I also think he knew that going home and leaving the army in my past was what was best for me.

I walked through the airport with my luggage in tow, my belly now sporting a little bump. I felt giddy to be getting back to my home, but nervous that it wouldn't feel like home any longer.

We touched down in Belize and I could see a helicopter, a final gift from the US Army. A free ride to the little island off the coast. I was home, and I was ready for the best adventure, to be a mom.

As we drove toward my house, I thought excitedly about watching my baby playing in the surf, and races to the lighthouse. My thoughts were interrupted by the sound of the tires on a cobblestone driveway. I looked out the window at the white house staring back at me, an old friend asking where I had been. I thanked the driver, got my bags, and headed for the door.

As I unlocked the big black lock, I could smell the metal. The door creaked open like it hadn't been open in years instead of months. I stepped onto the marble floors, listening to the familiar sound of my shoes. There were boxes littering the entry way, I almost tripped on them. It was all my stuff that they had retrieved from Colonel Weaver's. I ran my hand over the boxes and counted my steps like I had done so many times before to memorize my surroundings. All the furniture was still there, covered with big white sheets; the house smelled of stale air and dust.

I walked to the bedroom, there were no remnants of the things that had happened, just waves of white cloth, a ghost town in many ways. I looked forward to the challenge of making it a home again. I walked back toward the extra bedroom and stood in the doorway. It was cold and medical, so I closed my eyes and was imagining a crib and a rocking chair when I heard a noise from the kitchen.

"Please don't be a snake," I said out loud.

I walked out of the hall into the dining room and a familiar shadow was standing there, I closed my eyes hard, thinking I was hallucinating, then he stepped out of the shadows. I stared at him, incredulous, and put my hands to my mouth in disbelief.

Holding a small glass of orange juice in one hand and a cane in the other he smiled and asked, "Are you okay?"

"Are you real," my eyes searching every inch of his face, "or a ghost sent to torment me? How is this possible?"

"They got to Sidney Gains; without Colonel Weaver there to intimidate him he cracked and told them everything. But we can discuss that another day."

He set the orange juice down on the table next to him and walked with his cane toward me. I couldn't move, I wasn't sure any of this was really happening. When he got to me, he struggled to kneel down. He placed his hands on my belly.

"You are so beautiful," he said, gazing up at me.

I couldn't help it; tears were streaming down my face.

"It's his," I said, hesitating to say any more.

"I know," he said. "I would be honored to raise my brother's baby as my own. He was once a good man, the devil came for him, but I loved him just the same."

A sob escaped into the air.

"Will you let me take care of you two?"

The sob turned to laughter, and I wiped the tears away.

"Ask me again," I said.

He paused for a moment, and his expression told me he knew what I had meant, and he smiled.

"Are you okay?"

"We are now."

Epilogue
Family

I lay there by candlelight, the flickers dancing shadows off the walls. The storm had knocked out the power. I rubbed my hands across my swollen belly and listened. The rain pelted the tile roof, thunder rolled in the distance and waves crashed outside. The door opened and Will walked in holding a candle in one hand, he still had a limp but managed to get rid of his cane.

"He is back in bed, but he's afraid of the storm," he said, walking over to the other side of the bed.

I rolled to face him and gave him the best puppy-dog eyes I could manage, sticking my bottom lip out into a full pout.

"He will never learn if we just go get him," he scolded, expertly ignoring my attempts.

Just then the door creaked, I saw a little eyeball peering through a crack in the door. I looked at him again with pleading eyes.

"Alright," he said in defeat.

"Hank, buddy," I said.

My little blond, curly haired boy poked his head through the door. I opened my blanket inviting him in, and he ran and climbed into bed with me cradling around my belly.

"Is baby sister scared too?" he asked.

"Not anymore, buddy, not anymore."

About the Author

T.C. Grantham is a 40 year old mother of 4 children (Hopefully 1 more, she says!).

When she is not being a mom she is a Photographer, a Doula, and a Hairstylist, and now a Published Author!

She lives in Utah, USA and has been married to her childhood sweetheart for 23 years. It was him who pushed her to finish and publish her debut novel.

Made in the USA
Monee, IL
27 August 2023

41700996R00152